Interlude with the Vampire!

Steele shrugged and turned to his master. "Okay, boss, what do you want me to do?" he asked of the vampire.

The vampire grinned. "I want this cell of resistance found and crushed. You can have whatever you need, resources, men, anything."

"Are these the same guys who kicked your ass last month?" Steele asked innocently.

The look Nero gave him was beyond withering, and he wondered briefly if he had finally gone too far. He was surprised to note that he almost wished he had. The last few years in the mercenary business had made him tired and lately he had begun to yearn for something, he wasn't sure what, but he felt empty inside. No, it was more that. He felt incomplete. This sort of thing had never happened to him before. Whatever it was, he didn't like how it felt. He was aware of pushing his vampire masters that little bit further of late, but couldn't really bring himself to care.

"You tread a very thin line, human," Nero warned. "I hope that you are still smiling at the completion of this mission. If you fail, believe me, I will enjoy watching you beg for death…"

VAMPIRE APOCALYPSE

A World Torn Asunder

DEREK GUNN

Black Death Books
An imprint of
KHP Industries
www.khpindustries.com

Dedication

In life we encounter many changes, both ordered and chaotic.
I am fortunate to have found my anchor in this maelstrom.
This book is dedicated to my wife, Alice, with all my love.
Thank you.

VAMPIRE APOCALYPSE:
A WORLD TORN ASUNDER
by
DEREK GUNN

Black Death Books
is an imprint of
KHP Industries
http://www.khpindustries.com

ISBN: 0-9767914-8-X

Cover art by KHP Studios

10 9 8 7 6 5 4 3 2 1

PROLOGUE

The Beginning of the End

T he town slept. A shroud of darkness lay heavily over everything like an impenetrable blanket except for the occasional glow of dull light from oil lamps that dotted the scene and seemed to mirror the pinpricks of light in the sky above. The massive turbines that used to pump out power for the whole state had ground to a halt more than a month earlier as the last reserves of fuel had dried up. The few wind- or water-powered plants were overloaded and their use was rigidly restricted to emergency and local authority use.

Jack Newton sighed as he watched over his dying hometown. States with nuclear power stations fared much better but they no longer fed the power grids of surrounding states, unless those poorer states were prepared to pay exorbitant prices. These power states had already begun to grow more dominant, placing guards on their borders to prevent mass migrations. It wasn't that they didn't allow people to relocate, but that they wanted to choose those who would be allowed to do so. The talented, those who would be useful in this new world, were welcomed and all others were left to scrape a living in the poorer, dying states.

The Central Government had quickly lost its influence as local militia were called in to protect each state's assets. A once proud, united nation rapidly fell into a feudal system where few were rich in the new source of wealth: power. Or, at least, power that did not require oil to run its turbines, natural resources, and, most importantly, a plentiful supply of food. Many waited as other states were forced to give up what valuables they had—their brightest people, fertile land or mineral rights—in order to receive a trickle of power to keep their people warm for the coming winter.

It hadn't taken long for an advanced civilisation to regress to such a state. A brief but vicious war in the Middle East had laid waste to the world's oil fields and left what remained under a cloud of radioactivity that would take decades to dissipate. Millions had died. Whole countries had been wiped off the map, and agreements between countries had stretched and then broken as accusations and blame were tossed around in the aftermath.

Europe closed ranks against a resurging Russia and a dominant China. America, fearful of loosing its foothold in Europe, had sided with the new Franco-British alliance, expending huge amounts of precious resources, both in materials and manpower, in skirmishes that threatened to escalate to total war but always seemed to stop just in time.

The massive drain on stockpiles along with a change in public opinion at home as rationing became widespread, eventually took its toll and America was forced to pull back and allow the sheer numbers of the Russian/Chinese alliance to swarm over a ravaged Europe. Six months it had taken, from the first shot, to redraw the world map and change an entire civilisation. Nations that were once poor because of their lack of technical advancement now reigned supreme in a world where sheer numbers again counted for more than technological advancements that were no longer viable in a world without the power to operate them.

Newton pulled his sheepskin jacket tighter around him as the cold sucked greedily at his body and left him shivering. He could see a glow on the horizon where the neighbouring state still pumped power to its towns and cities from their nuclear plant. The lines that connected his city to the plant were still there, but the power that ran through them was strictly rationed and paid for with everything of value that the state had.

They had already sold off all usable land around their borders in advance to cover themselves for the minimum power requirements to see them through the coming winter. But God only knew what they would do then. They had already lost their top researchers in their chemical and steel industries. He couldn't really blame them; they had families to feed and the offer of a guaranteed future in a richer state was hard to turn down.

There were already rumblings in the town meetings of using their own local militia to take the power plant by force; they had provided most of the muscle and resources in its construction anyway and only a few miles and a now contentious state line separated it from their own control. The plant was actually closer to this city than it was to their nearest centre of population and had more than enough power to spare for everybody's needs.

Unfortunately, on his last sweep of the area, Newton had noticed that a new military camp had been set up around the plant and armoured vehicles now patrolled the entire area. He had been shocked that relations had degraded to such a level. *How quickly they forget*, he thought.

The crackle of the radio startled him from his reverie and he turned reluctantly and leaned into the patrol car, snatched at the radio and cursed as it got tangled on the barrel of his shotgun.

"Go ahead, Lou," he said as he turned back towards the city.

"Chief, we've got another one."

Newton ran a hand over his face, massaging his temples as he felt a headache throb at the back of his eyes. *Dear God, what is going on?*

"Where?" he snapped.

"Over by the Grady's place, I've sent Phil and Jess over already."

"Okay, I'll meet them there, out." He tossed the radio into the passenger seat and climbed into the car, taking a moment to rearrange his gun belt. He had had to tighten the belt by another notch yesterday, and it was still a little loose. The rationing did have at least one positive result and he had felt more alive in the last few weeks than he could remember. As police chief it was his responsibility to hold things together, and where he had grown lazy before the troubles in a town where little happened, he was now stretched too thin in a town that was falling apart.

Increasingly he had reports from parents that their children had disappeared; he dutifully investigated but found nothing. He assumed that the lure of the larger cities, those that promised food and power, had just been too much for some to ignore. Dwindling food and resources and a total lack of prospects for the future of the town were strong factors when those young people were deciding their future. Those that had stronger family ties tended to remain, but the community was populated primarily with people older than would be needed for the hard times ahead.

There had been ten disappearances over the last few days, but with three riots, a few suicides and gang fights as the youths that did remain saw their opportunity to expand their own power bases, he had little time to devote to them. And now, on top of all that, he had a serial killer. A particularly vicious killer who was taking full advantage of the lack of power and the extended hours of darkness it afforded him. This would make the fourth victim in as many nights. He shivered as he thought of the previous victims and how they had been ripped apart.

He took a left into Wyndell Road, slowing at the now darkened traffic lights at the crossroads before accelerating through onto Fairfield. It was unlikely anyone else was driving as fuel for vehicles had been rationed now for quite some time, but it didn't hurt to be careful; even small accidents could be fatal with the hospital running so low on supplies.

Pat and Jillian Grady lived out by the mall on Route 40. They were a quiet couple, middle-aged with a teenage daughter. He had had reason to caution Jennifer Grady just last week when he had disturbed a late night party in the local cemetery. He had caught a group of them defacing gravestones.

It wasn't that she had actually been doing the damage but that she had been unlucky enough to have been caught with those who were. The kids that were left in town had few outlets for their frustration. Their nice, comfortable lives had been drastically changed with the rationing and most of them had been recruited to work the land around the town, trying to get it ready for spring planting. It was backbreaking work, clearing trees and scrub and then burning them and raking the ash into the soil for the nutrients, but it was essential to their survival. They hadn't caused that much damage, but a few headstones had been knocked over and two mausoleums had been broken into.

Jennifer's parents had been shocked but Newton had played it down with them; kids needed some outlets, and with no TV, no entertainment of any kind, and no alcohol, it was no surprise that they were frustrated.

He saw the flashing lights of the patrol car, pulled in behind it and made his way over to the small group of people ahead of him. Jess saw him approach and excused herself from a conversation with Peter Hackett, the Grady's neighbour and the town's sole remaining, and now redundant, computer specialist. All the other technical experts had left for the states that still had power to run their machines, but Hackett had been born in this town and at sixty-five was damned well going to die in it, or at least that was what he had told Jack when he had asked him after a particularly late session of the local council. Nothing had actually been decided at that meeting but he did recall that all twelve members of the council had passed out drunk, so it hadn't been a complete waste.

"What have we got, Jessie?" Jack asked as she reached him.

"It's the worst yet, Chief." Jess Walker was a handsome woman. She stood five-foot-five, with broad shoulders and a trim waist. At first glance she seemed quite ordinary, especially in a uniform that was designed to emphasise respect and not her physical attributes. But as he approached her Newton was momentarily struck by an intensity in her features that he had not noticed before. A mass of the deepest red curls Jack had ever seen defied her every attempt to imprison them beneath her patrol cap and strands burst out here and there, emphasising the paleness of her complexion. Her eyes were a dazzling green and they seemed to shine with an inner fire that belied her diminutive stature and held him in thrall for a moment before her voice snapped him out of it.

"There's four dead," she continued after she had taken a deep breath. "Sorry," she faltered again as the memory of the carnage caused bile to rise in her throat.

Jack laid his hand on her shoulder. "It's all right," he said quietly. "I'll check it out myself and we'll talk later. See if you can get a cup of coffee from one of the neighbours."

She nodded and Jack moved past her towards the Grady's house. The Grady family lived in a good part of town and the houses were all well cared for with small but neat lawns and two cars in every driveway, although with the current shortages these vehicles were of no use to anyone. The Grady's house was a bungalow, but was one of the few on the street that had an attic conversion, and the extension seemed to loom over him as he approached the door. *Four dead*, he thought. *Jesus, what have we got roaming our streets?*

After the second killing he had called the FBI for help, but they had let him know in no uncertain terms that they had enough to do without visiting every damned state that had a homicide. Ever since the power had gone, each state had pretty much been left to their own devices. It was impossible to govern or police a country the size of America when transport was reduced to horses and a few steam trains. Nuclear powered and solar powered vehicles were few and far between, and they were all used to strengthen the country's defenses against the threat of invasion from Russia and China, who seemed to have adapted much better to this new age. Newton doubted that either country would risk an invasion, it was such a long way from Europe by conventional means, but you never knew.

Jack shook himself from his reverie as he passed through the door. The first thing that struck him was the smell. It was a heady mix of excrement and a sickly sweet odour that caught in his throat and made him gag. He fumbled for his handkerchief to try and filter the stench but the flimsy material wasn't up to the task and he could feel the bile rise in his throat. He gulped air through his mouth, and while this helped him force the nausea down, the rank air dried his throat and started a coughing fit that forced him to breathe in small, careful breaths.

He took a moment to gather himself before continuing on into the house and made his way towards the glow of the gas lamp in the front room. The bodies, or rather what was left of them, were strewn about the room. Jack could see mangled flesh, bare bones and organs in the dull light, although mercifully the pale glow covered the worst of the atrocity in undulating shadows caused by the flickering of the flame as the wick began to run dry of the precious fuel.

The flame stuttered once more and then suddenly went out. Jack found himself alone in the room and forced down the urge to turn and run out. It wouldn't do for the others to see him like that and he'd probably break his neck anyway. It still amazed him how dark it was now that streetlights no longer provided a background glow. It was pitch dark in the room, so much so that he could not see anything at all. There wasn't even a faint glow from outside and for a moment he lost his bearings. *Which way was he facing? Was the door behind him or to his right?* He felt his pulse quicken and the darkness felt like it was closing in on him, as if it was alive and was coiling around him ready to squeeze the life out of him.

Newton clenched his teeth and forced himself to breath normally as he retraced his steps in his mind. He was fairly certain that he had not turned in any direction since he had entered the room so the door should be directly behind him. He turned slowly, pointedly ignoring the grisly scenes that he imagined all. around him. He forced himself to breathe through his mouth and slid his feet forward until he reached the door, and then quickened his step until he felt the cool air from outside wash over him.

His skin prickled and he shivered, though whether it was from the sudden chill or the images that still danced through his mind he couldn't be sure. He assumed that three of the dead would be Pat and Jillian Grady and their daughter Jennifer, but who was the fourth? He put that mystery to one side as he approached Jess again. She had obviously found a kindly neighbour and now sat against her patrol car with her hands wrapped around a steaming mug. He thought of the mangled remains in the house and offered up silent thanks that it wouldn't be him that had to shift through the bodies to identify them.

Jess looked a lot better. Her cheeks had small red blushes where the steam of the drink wafted upwards, and she looked sheepish as she saw Jack approach.

"Sorry about that," she began but Jack waved it off.

"Nothing to apologise for," he interrupted. "I feel queasy myself. Any more of that coffee?" he asked as the pungent aroma reached him.

She handed over a flask and a mug and Jack continued as he poured. "What have we got?"

Jess put down her mug and riffled through the pages in her notebook until she found what she was looking for. "We got a call from Peter Hackett, that's the neighbour, at 2:05 this morning."

Jack looked down at his watch and saw the luminous dials show 3:15.

"He was very agitated, according to dispatch," she continued. "He described the screaming from next door as terrifying."

"That's a strange word to use to describe what could have been a domestic disturbance," Jack interrupted.

"I thought that too," Jess agreed. "He rushed out from his house as we pulled up but insisted he hadn't gone into the house when I asked him, said he was too scared. After seeing the carnage inside, I can't say that I blame him. Anyway, he said that he had never heard anything so ear-piercing or as frightening in all his life. The screams woke him up and went on for a good ten minutes, said he only summoned up the courage to call us when all went quiet again."

"Anyone else hear the noises?"

"We're checking now with the other neighbours but the Smiths are away and the next house is a good way down the street."

Jack grunted. He had known Peter Hackett for years and didn't suspect that he had anything to do with the killings, for one thing he didn't have the strength needed to rip bodies apart like that, but he wanted to make sure that all the bases were covered. There had been no new faces that he was aware of in town in the last few months so it was more likely that these killings were being done by someone that he knew.

The thought made him sick. How could any human being tear people apart like that, let alone someone he knew, someone he may have shared a joke with or held a door open for.

He shivered.

"Okay," he sighed, "seal up the house and wait for Doc Sallis." They didn't have a forensic department, and didn't have any power to run one even if they had, so Doctor Jim Sallis, formally retired but pressed back into service when his young replacement decided to jump state, was the best they could do. Jack ran his hands through his thinning hair, *God damn it; this is no way to run an investigation.*

"Simmer down!" Dan Fogarty banged a wooden gavel on the podium in front of him repeatedly in a vain effort to be heard amid the bedlam in the hall. The air was thick with smoke, both from cigarettes and from the numerous gas lamps placed on both sides of the hall and along its length. Smoking had had a huge uptake in the past few months and Fogarty was worried about what they would do when the town's supply ran out. It was already dangerously low and tobacco commanded a high price with the mobile traders that visited more and more infrequently. His over-active imagination had already played out the horrors of a whole town suffering cold turkey at the same time.

Anyway, one problem at a time, he thought as he pushed away that potential problem in favour of the one at hand. He looked out over the sea of faces. Many of them were familiar, all of them were scared. He banged his gavel again.

"Please, we have a lot to get through!" he shouted aloud, but far from the volume his deep voice could command if needed, and slowly the room came to order. He smiled to himself, pleased that he was still able to control a room. He had been mayor for 5 years now, since before the current problems, and liked to think that he had no small part in keeping the community together in a country where bigger towns were already deserted. They didn't really have much going for them as a town in this new world; they had no power, little fertile or grazing land left that they had not already bartered, but somehow the community had stayed together. They had enough food for the coming winter and had organised enough power from the nuclear plant to see them through the worst of the weather, but it had taken the last of their good livestock and all the land around their border. They would have very little left for next year and beyond.

On top of all this they now seemed to have a serial killer amongst them. This was something that scared the people more than any of their other worries. They could fight against the hunger and the cold by working hard, rationing and preparing less fertile land for next year's harvest. How could they protect themselves against a killer that seemed to choose his victims randomly and with impunity?

In every case so far there had been no sign of forced entry, and yet the bodies had been ripped apart as if by an animal, although Doctor Sallis had assured him that this was not the work of an animal. He sighed. He had decided to call this meeting and lay all the information out to the town's inhabitants; he felt he owed them that much.

"Alright," he continued. "I've asked Doc Sallis to say a few words tonight, so if you have any questions about the killings you'll be able to ask him yourselves. Just remember that we have children here tonight so don't go scaring them any more than they already are. Sheriff Newton is also here," he nodded to the front row where the Sheriff sat beside the aforementioned doctor, "so he'll give you an update on the investigation itself.

"I have asked them both to give you all the information they have, so there will be no cover-up or keeping anything from you for your own good. We're in this together and I feel I owe you that much. However, I warn you now that I want this meeting to be orderly." He paused as he scanned the sea of faces. "I know most of you are armed, and I can't blame you for that, but anyone getting out of hand will be dealt with quickly. I remind you again that there are children here. Now, with that said, I'll pass you over to our good doctor."

Fogarty nodded to the Doctor and stepped down from the podium. There was a nervous shuffle of feet around the room and a few coughs as people settled themselves and this in turn sparked off a chorus of shushing as Sallis laid his notes on the podium. Doc Sallis was a small, overweight man with receding hair and a pinched face that seemed more at home with a scowl than a smile. Despite this, the man was well liked and his outward appearance was in total contrast to the man beneath the skin. He might have the look of a grump but he was in fact a jovial man that people found easy to relate to and was a particular favourite with the children. He had been the town doctor for the last forty years and despite being past retirement age had continued in the role without complaint. He was well respected but the hush that settled over the audience had more to do with his ashen appearance than anything else.

"Friends," he began, his deep voice cracking slightly under the intense scrutiny of the audience, "I must confess that I am not entirely sure where to start." He smiled weakly before continuing. "As you know there have been four incidents over the last week. I will leave it to our Sheriff to explain the details surrounding the deaths; I will limit myself to the method. I am mindful of our younger citizens so please don't ask for specific details as I will not give them. If you feel compelled to delve into the unsavoury details you can ask me later." The look he cast around the audience left no one in any doubt that they would want a very good reason to ask for those details.

"The victims were all killed in the same way—that is, death was caused by massive trauma and blood loss. In short, they were torn apart. The strength needed for this was far beyond what one would expect from a human being."

"Does that mean we're dealing with an animal?" The question came from the centre of the room and Doc Sallis squinted through the smoky haze to identify the speaker.

"No, John, it does not," he replied, identifying the town's local Century representative. "No animal would kill like this without eating some of the victim, or at the very least leaving teeth marks on the remains. These poor people were torn apart for reasons other than food or territorial dispute, so that lays my suspicions firmly at the door of humanity, I'm afraid."

"But you said that the strength needed was too much for a human, Doctor."

"For a normal human, yes. However, these days there are so many drugs and enhancements available that the human body is quite capable of amazing feats over limited periods. We are dealing with someone very sick but very clever. There are no forensics left at the scene, at least none that I can process with our limited resources. There is no sign of forced entry, and seemingly no pattern, all the victims were unrelated as far as we can see."

"Did they know their killer?"

The question was a simple one but the implications it carried immediately silenced the low hush of whispers that had begun as everyone waited for an answer.

"That is a good question but I'm afraid I'm not the one to answer it. I think this is a good point to hand over to our Sheriff."

Newton nodded and approached the podium. He was all too aware that every eye in the building was on him and he forced himself to breath evenly as he turned to face the crowd. He was good with people, but on a one-to-one basis. Crowds were a totally different matter, and petrified crowds were even worse.

"We have a small community here, one that's growing smaller in the current climate. There have been no visitors to the town for at least two weeks, no sightings of vagrants, traveling peddlers or officials in or near the town at all. I am not aware of any people who have recently come to live here, or indeed any who are visiting friends or families. Each victim was found in their home with no obvious signs of forced entry and no evidence of robbery." He paused briefly and then sighed, "I suppose what I'm trying to say is that all evidence so far indicates that the killer was known to each of the victims."

A gasp rippled through the audience. People looked around them fearfully as if looking for someone with a sign over their head proclaiming them to be the killer. In seconds a community united in fear and hardship became a dysfunctional collection of smaller groups as families closed ranks, individuals were ostracised and women pulled their children closer and looked with suspicion at any male in the room. Chairs screeched across hard wooden floors as people began to physically replicate the groups that their minds had already created. All this happened in seconds; years of community building were shattered through fear and mistrust.

"Order!" The word was followed by the gavel pounding on the podium and everyone's attention was drawn back to

Newton as he raised the gavel for another strike only to freeze and lower it gently as order was restored.

"Sit down!" he shouted as people used to a quiet, mild-mannered Sheriff flopped immediately into their chairs in shock. "I must admit that I counseled against telling you that but our good mayor has more faith in you and your ties as a community than I have. How dare you. This is exactly what the killer wants. By dividing us he makes it easier for him to find new victims. The only way to beat him is to remain united. He can't kill us all if we stay together."

"Oh I don't know about that."

The words came from the back of the hall and carried with them an icy wind that poured through the open doors. A figure stood just inside the doors, and as people turned to look they noticed other figures dart quickly into the hall and fan out behind the figure.

"Who the hell are you?" Fogarty stood and faced the figure, his voice loud and strong, although the slightly higher pitch betrayed his fear.

"Oh my God, it's Johnnie," a woman towards the back of the hall shrieked and rose with open arms and hurried towards one of the figures at the back of the hall. Her husband rose and grabbed at her but she pulled away and stumbled towards the figure.

Newton placed his hand on his holstered gun and moved away from the podium.

"Who are you?" His tone carried with it a quiet authority and menace that many of the people present had never heard before. His eyes flicked briefly at Jess and he nodded once and then looked directly at the central figure. Jess moved to the side to ensure she had a clear view and brought her hand up to her radio and spoke in low tones.

"Mary, stay back" Newton ordered but the woman paid no attention and continued towards the figure where she threw her arms around him and buried her face in the figure's chest. The boy remained motionless and the whole room stilled as if a pause button had been pressed. The woman's sobs continued but suddenly she began to retch. Her hand came up to her lips but was too late to prevent the bile from spewing from her mouth. Her sobs became whimpers as she doubled over and gasped for air. She looked at the figure quizzically, her hand pressed firmly against her mouth and nose. The object of her attention looked over at the figure in the centre and raised an eyebrow. The figure nodded once and the thing that had been Johnnie smiled.

The audience couldn't really see clearly and were still getting over the shock of the abrupt appearance of these strange figures. The sudden scream from the back of the room startled everyone. Johnnie grabbed the woman who had raised him and tore her throat out, sucking greedily at the spurting blood before letting her body fall to the ground.

Newton couldn't tell what had happened but he saw the crowd at the back begin to surge away from the figures at the end of the hall. He pulled his gun from its holster and fired a round into the air. For the third time that night the crowd froze. Too much had happened to destroy their peaceful existence. The gun shot stopped them initially but the smell coming from the back of the room soon had people pushing back again, albeit more slowly.

There was a clear fifteen feet between the figures and the last line of the audience and Newton moved down the stage steps and pushed his way through to the empty area. He held his gun firmly on the figure and noted Jess taking up position to his left. His eyes flicked briefly to Mary's body and he scanned the faces of the figures. He recognised all ten of the missing boys and was about to repeat his question when the smell hit him.

He felt bile rise up his throat as the odour reached him. It was sickly sweet, cloying and foul all at once. He concentrated on the central figure again and forced himself to be calm. He heard the sound of sirens wailing as he saw two patrol cars pull up outside, and he straightened a little taller as he saw his men approach through the open door.

"Okay, Johnnie, you're under arrest. Come over here and kneel on the floor now." His tone was controlled but he was petrified. *What the hell was going on? A kid he had known for years had just ripped his mother's throat out and just stood calmly as if he had merely taken a bite from a sandwich. Who was the guy in the centre and what the hell was that smell?* The questions ran through his mind threatening to overpower him but he forced them all aside and tried to control the situation by using his training.

"On the ground now," he repeated more forcefully and tightened his finger on the trigger.

"Sheriff," the figure spoke quietly, "this is really quite pointless, you know." The man's soft, almost whispered, voice sent a shiver down Newton's back. Maybe it was the cold that swept through the open doors that had his body shaking so badly, but he was truthful enough to admit to himself that it was unlikely. His hands were sweating, making him tighten his grip on the gun, and he clamped his teeth tightly together to hide the fact that they had begun to chatter. He knew himself well enough to know that he wasn't a coward. He couldn't actually pin it down; maybe it was the figure's apparent indifference to having a gun pointed at him, or the way he commanded the attention of everyone in the room, or even the stench of death that emanated from him. But he could admit to himself that this man terrified him.

"Cover me!" he nodded to Jess and the deputies that had taken station at the door. He approached Johnnie and almost threw up on the spot. He hadn't actually seen what had happened before, as his attention had been divided between all the figures, so it was only as he reached the young man that he could see the blood running down his mouth.

Johnnie smiled at him, revealing long sharp teeth.

Newton suddenly and viciously brought his weapon up and across Johnnie's face. He knew that he had surprised them as the figure had to bark a command to keep the others from attacking him. Johnnie hit the ground hard but was back on his feet faster than Newton could see. He felt the boy's hand grip his throat like a vice and suddenly found himself dangling in mid air as his lungs gasped for air.

His felt light-headed and spots of light danced in his vision. He dimly heard a shot and felt himself crumple to the floor. He heard a second command from the stranger and could almost feel the hatred emanating from the other nine boys.

"Are you all right, Chief?" Newton pulled himself to his feet and nodded to Jess as she offered her help. It was only when he was standing again that he noticed that Johnnie was on the ground. He had assumed that Jess had fired a shot in the air but as he looked down at the figure he noticed a neat hole in his forehead.

"Some shot," he noted and retrieved his own weapon. "Now I..."

He was interrupted by a shuffling on the floor and he paled as he saw Johnnie stir and then rise to his feet. The blood oozing from the wound dried to a trickle and then stopped altogether as the flesh around the wound began to close and knit together as he watched.

"Oh shit," his voice croaked through his damaged throat. He pulled the trigger and fired directly into Johnnie's heart. He felt the gun buck in his hands and saw the impact as blood spurted from the wound. Johnnie staggered back but didn't fall and Newton fired twice more before he finally realised that it wasn't doing any good.

"Do you see now, Sheriff?" the figure smiled at him. Newton was dimly aware of the growing unease in the crowd behind him. The situation was a hair trigger away from total chaos. He had no idea what was going on but he knew that whatever these men were, they weren't human. The wrong move now would probably lead to total slaughter. His mind was in turmoil, impossible thoughts of vampires and demons pulled at his sanity, but everyone in the room was looking to him for direction. He was damned if he would let them die for nothing. The creatures, or whatever they were, had consciously not attacked them as yet, despite the gunshots, and there must be a reason for that. The figure in the centre was obviously the leader and had total control of the boys. If there was any way out of this it was through him.

"What's all this about Mr...?"

"Names are unimportant," the figure smiled, "they are meaningless nonsense created by a short lived race who spends too much of its limited life trying to become immortal in name if not actuality. We have no need for them."

"What exactly is it that you do need?"

"Right now," the stranger continued, "in thousands of towns all over the world, vampires such as myself are quietly taking this world away from your kind. One by one the towns will fall to us and then we will begin on the cities. By the time you even notice it will be too late."

The news hit Newton like a blow. His mind raced as pieces of the puzzle fell into place. "Then the killings ..."

"Were a necessary distraction, yes." The stranger finished. "Despite what Hollywood may tell you the first few days of a vampire's existence are a critical time. They are weak as kittens as the change ravages their bodies. As you can see, it is short lived."

"Why tell us this? You obviously have the advantage, why not just slaughter us and move on?"

"Unlike you humans, we vampires are a patient race. We have hidden for centuries from your kind because we could see that you humans were dangerous. Because you are so short lived you achieve amazing advances in short time frames. It was decided long ago that this advancement, or technology as you have dubbed it, would be dangerous to us. Over the centuries we ensured that all references to our race were removed and those that could not be removed were ridiculed and reduced to myth."

"We bided our time, but now that technology has stagnated we will come from the shadows and take what is ours."

"All very interesting but why are you telling us this?" Newton was sure there was an advantage here, something that could very well allow them to bargain for some or all of their lives. He just had to find it.

"In order to spread throughout the world we need two things: food and security"

Newton felt sick as realisation dawned on him. "You want us to sign on to your army."

"In a sense. The food element we can satisfy now by killing all here; however, who knows what will happen next week or next month? Who knows when such a feast will again present itself to us? We could kill you and carry the dead with us, but blood sours quite quickly."

"You want us to become a mobile blood bank for you." Newton gasped as the full horror hit him. "You're insane if you think we would stoop that low. What could you possibly offer..." He snapped his jaw shut, wishing he could take back his last question, already knowing that he had played into the vampire's hands.

"I'm glad you asked." The stranger turned from Newton and faced the petrified crowd. "You have heard what I have said so far. Your race is already defeated but you don't have to die, your children don't have to be tortured or killed. I can offer some of you power beyond your imagination, immortality and land after the coming war is over. To others I offer places of favour in our elite guard. Places of power where you can walk in daylight but will have power near to our own and access to pleasures beyond your imaginations. To those who give their allegiance to us we will spare their families and allow them to live in peace. To all others you will die here tonight."

The room was totally silent and Newton turned and looked over the townspeople.

"You know you can't trust him. He will take you with him and drink you dry only to cast you aside like a bottle off a shelf." Newton could see husbands whispering to their wives, men and women standing alone with their eyes glazed, thinking of the promised pleasures, and knew that too many were already beyond reason. The first of them tentatively moved forward and Newton raised his gun and fired.

The bullet tore a hole in the floor just in front of the lead man. "Don't do it, Jack," Newton warned. "You can't trust them."

"They're going to kill us anyway, Sheriff. You heard him. At least this way Jenny and little Jack might have a chance," Jack Thompson pleaded. Newton knew that Thompson wasn't a bad man but they had to see that the only way to beat the vampires was in not helping them now when they were still weak.

"Jack, they can't exist during the day, they'll never win as long as they have to hide away every day. If we help them now then the whole world is finished. What kind of future are you leaving for little Jack if they win?"

"Sheriff, you don't have kids, how would you know what it's like to let someone threaten him? God forgive me but I just can't let them tear him apart."

"Not even to save the world?" Newton asked as the weight of his gun suddenly became too much and he lowered the weapon.

"Not even for that." Thompson lowered his head and walked slowly over to the vampires. About half of the younger fathers followed him and almost all the young men that had remained in the town. Newton saw two of his deputies shrug and holster their guns and join the growing group. Newton wasn't angry at the fathers but he shot looks of pure hatred at the single men for their betrayal.

He jumped suddenly as he felt a hand slide into his and turned to see Jess lean forward to kiss him on the cheek. There were tears in her eyes and something else, something he really should have seen before. *God, was I that blind?* He thought as he looked at his deputy. *I never realised, never even recognised the signs. All that time alone and she was in front of me all the time.*

He put his arm around her and squeezed. He saw the stranger indicate that the families of the men should exit through the still open door. The women and children didn't need further prompting and soon the hall was mostly empty.

Newton looked around at those that remained. Most were too old to be tempted by this devil's promises, but some were not. Some parents stood protectively in front of their young charges. Sons and daughters, old enough to make up their own minds, stood in contrast in front of their parents, petrified but defiant. Tears rolled down Newton's cheek. It should be quick, at least.

The creature looked at Newton with a quizzical look. "What do you hope to gain by dying?" he asked.

Newton looked at him. "The fact that you have to ask means that you are already defeated."

The creature shrugged and left. His leaving was like a lever releasing a spring and the ten remaining creatures surged forward.

Outside the survivors couldn't bear to look at each other and remained huddled in the cold air, alone with their thoughts, until the screaming inside died away.

CHAPTER
ONE

H arris winced. A cramp shot up his leg and he shifted his position to get more comfortable in his treetop perch. He brought the binoculars to his eyes and surveyed the front of the house. The two-story Georgian structure was richly covered in blooming ivy and nestled in the middle of its 100-acre estate. From his vantage point, Harris could see the large wooden entrance doors set behind sun bleached sandstone pillars.

Those doors, he knew, led to the main hall and the large stairway that spiraled upward to the 10 bedrooms above. The dining room, lounge and servants' quarters covered the lower floor. The grounds, once well kept, had grown wild and untidy in later years. Plants which had once provided colourful splashes against the green canvas now spilled chaotically over the beds and added to the tangle of the overgrown grass.

"Blue Leader, initiate in 5 minutes." Harris spoke softly into the microphone positioned directly in front of his mouth. His headset broadcasted the message clearly to his colleagues around the grounds.

Harris suppressed the nervousness in the pit of his stomach. He transferred the machine gun that hung from a strap on his back to his lap. As the seconds crawled by, he picked out his targets: three single patrols between his position and the house, and the two guards at the doors. He ignored the others, confident his team members would take care of them. He checked his watch, eager to begin the assault, and then slipped down from the tree. The last seconds ticked by and Harris reached for a grenade on his utility belt.

". . .two, one."

Harris counted down the last seconds and pulled the pin on the grenade. He reached back and threw it towards the nearest of his targeted patrols. The guards barely had time to register the dull thud of the grenade landing behind them before it exploded and their bodies were thrown into the air to land in crumpled heaps some feet away. Harris launched himself from cover and sprinted towards the house, firing as he ran.

His hail of bullets tore into the second patrol before they could fully react and their bodies jerked spasmodically with each impact. Explosions and gunfire could be heard all around him as the rest of his team joined the action. Harris leapt to the ground, narrowly avoiding a hail of bullets that pierced the air where he had stood only seconds before. He rolled and brought his weapon up and emptied the rest of the magazine into the last of his targeted patrols.

Harris knelt to change the magazine and looked around. To the east he could see Johnson and his team running in relays of two as they covered each other on the approach to the house. Kelly and his team had taken the main gate and were already removing the bodies of the guards and opening the gates to let Jenkins and the rest of the trucks into the estate.

Harris glanced at his watch and then sprinted to the left side of the house. 3:05. *Not bad*, he thought. *Ahead of schedule.*

Harris plucked a second grenade from his belt, threw it at the main doors, and dove for cover. The explosion ripped the main doors from their hinges and sent a deadly hail of splinters into the face of the guard who had fired at him.

"How goes it?" a voice asked from behind a tree to his left.

Harris' heart lurched in his chest. "Shit!" He snapped his face sideways and saw Johnson. "You scared the crap out of me."

Johnson grinned, and then let loose a long burst into a group of three guards who appeared around the corner.

"Cover me!" Harris shouted. He ran up to the main doors and threw another grenade into the hall. Dust and plaster flew through the doorway as the grenade exploded. The window above them shattered and they dived to the ground to avoid the deadly glass and wood shrapnel.

"Right, in we go," Harris said. The two men rose, checked their magazines, and eased into the smoke.

Harris rolled to the floor as bullets ripped through the air above him. He returned fire in the direction of the assault and heard a scream before the enemy fire abruptly stopped. Johnson's team appeared behind him and Harris took the opportunity to reload. He watched as Johnson led his team to the stairs and proceeded up in the same leapfrog relay he had seen them perform outside. Two trucks pulled up outside the house and three more men jumped from the vehicles.

"Anderson!" Harris screamed over the noise of gunfire. "Take your men and clear out this floor."

Anderson nodded and the three men moved through the house, systematically clearing each room. Harris pulled a cigar from his shirt pocket and lit it.

Not many of these left now, he thought, and he drew the smoke into his lungs.

"All clear up here," someone said.

"Okay," Harris replied. He looked up the stairs to where Johnson had shouted. "Lets get to the basement and finish up before help gets here."

Johnson and his men ran down the stairs and made for the basement door under the stairs. The house was now burning in places and the smoke made visibility difficult. Johnson smashed through the basement door and grunted as a bullet ripped through his upper left arm. Harris pushed past him, threw another grenade down the stairs and ducked back into the hallway. The explosion shook the floor and he had to grab the door for support to avoid falling. Using the wall as protection Harris peered into the cellar. No shots came, but the cellar was pitch dark and Harris couldn't see any light switch.

"Get me a torch!" he shouted, and turned to his friend. "You okay, Johnson?"

"Yeah, went clean through. Hurts like a bitch, though."

Harris grinned with relief and looked up as Anderson returned with the torch. "Right, let's get this done."

Later Harris walked out to the garden. The sun burned into his body and he squinted along the line of his men. All of them were dirty from the smoke, some grasped various bleeding limbs, but all of them had the same look of determination.

At their feet lay seven coffins.

That basement held more of them than I expected, Harris thought.

"Burn the bastards," he said.

The men whooped and set about ripping the lids off the coffins. Harris looked impassively at the coffin nearest him. One of the men ripped the lid off and sunlight bathed the body within. The creature sat bolt upright and smoke began to wisp from the exposed flesh. It opened its eyes suddenly and Harris could almost feel the malevolence of its stare. Its skin puckered and blistered, stretched and split under the merciless assault of the afternoon sun. It tried to rise from the coffin, but pieces of flesh came away from the bone and bubbled like oil in a frying pan as it fell to the grass.

The screams in the garden were horrendous. The seven creatures thrashed and kicked in agony as they melted in front of the men. Harris looked around and saw another creature half out of its coffin. It was trying to pull itself into the shade of a nearby tree when the sun burnt though its hand and seared it at the wrist.

The creature fell forward and out of the coffin where the sun continued to char it until all that was left was smoking clothes and a pool of putrefying flesh. The faint wail of sirens reached the group as the last of the creatures died.

"Okay, we're finished here," Harris said. "Let's go."

The men picked up their gear and moved to the trucks. Harris paused briefly to drop a small note next to the coffins and then jumped up into the passenger seat of the first vehicle.

In the distance the sirens grew louder.

CHAPTER
TWO

"*What?*"

The word reverberated around the room. The sheer volume of the exclamation caused five of the six men present to jump and squirm uncomfortably. The six sat around a heavy, dark oak table that measured some twelve feet in length and five in width. The room was spacious, but completely bereft of any other furniture. The stark interior only served to emphasise the size of the room, and the bare walls amplified the thunderous report as it echoed around the terrified men.

Tony Williams fidgeted nervously in his chair. He looked down at the papers on the table in front of him, but knew that all eyes were directed at him. It had been his news that had made his master explode with such anger. He took a second to swallow and nervously repeated his message.

"Romulus and his clan were killed this afternoon. His mansion was att—"

"Attacked," interrupted the figure at the head of the table. "Who would dare?" The angry figure spat the words out between pale lips drawn back over wickedly sharp teeth.

Williams felt warm liquid trickle down his leg when the figure leaned to within inches of his face. Fetid breath assaulted his senses and bile rose in his throat. He swallowed desperately to prevent his stomach from spewing its contents.

"We don't know," he stammered finally.

The creature moved in a blur. One minute it was leaning over the table toward him, the next it was beside him.

Williams felt the strength of its arms as fingers gripped his neck and lifted him level with its six-foot-three frame. He gasped for air, but only succeeded in drawing small painful breaths. The foul stench from the creature's mouth was finally too much for him and bile burned its way up his throat. Williams felt his lungs burn as the creature's vice-like grip blocked his airway and forced the bile back down.

"Romulus was one of the council." The creature stared hard into William's eyes. "Where were the guards?"

Williams was turning blue when the creature finally loosened its grip. He fell to the ground and the bile in his throat spewed onto the floor and down his suit. "Dead," he finally managed through his tortured throat.

"Dead?" the creature hissed incredulously. "How many guards did he have?"

"Twenty-five," Williams replied as he struggled to his feet. "They were slaughtered. Bodies everywhere. It was a very professional job. We arrived fifteen minutes after the silent alarm was set off in the house, but by that time the guards were all dead. Romulus and his clan had been dragged out in the garden, and the bastards who did it were nowhere to be seen."

The creature crossed back to its seat and sat in one fluid, catlike motion. Williams took the opportunity to stagger over to his place at the table.

"What about the serum records?"

Williams breathed a sigh as the creature turned its attention to Jack Norton, administrative head of the city. Williams saw Norton stiffen and grinned at the other man's misfortune. Norton took a manila folder from the pile in front of him, but before he could open it, the folder was torn from his hands.

"As you will see, all humans received their monthly quota on schedule…" Norton began.

"Don't give me that," the creature interrupted. "If they had received the serum they wouldn't be out ripping Romulus' house apart, now would they? I want a full investigation," he continued, not waiting for a reply. "Every one of these cattle is to be checked before and after each dose."

Williams saw Norton raise his arm and open his mouth as if to say something, but he seemed to have second thoughts and sat down quickly. Williams chuckled to himself. The sheer numbers involved in that undertaking made such an investigation impossible, but at least failure in this would take attention away from him.

"Lord Nero," Williams really did not want to interrupt the creature. He knew that he was lucky to be alive, but he also knew that there were worse things than a quick death. "We found this beside the coffins." He leaned forward and offered the card.

Nero snapped the card so quickly Williams didn't realise the note was gone until the creature was unfolding it. He watched it examine the neat flowing script and he tensed as he waited for its reaction. Williams had looked at the note earlier, when he had found it at the scene, and he fully expected the creature to fly into a rage.

Instead the creature smiled a horrible, grotesque smile, and crumpled the note. "I want two hundred humans rounded up at random for tomorrow night. These heroes," Nero spat the word sarcastically, "will be shown the consequences of their actions."

CHAPTER
THREE

T he early morning sun began its laborious journey of the new day. Its rays, weak from the early hour, fought with the myriad shadows that still dominated the city. Harris easily assumed the slow, awkward gait of those around him and tried not to stare at the surrounding scenes of disrepair.

The vampires cared little for the living conditions of their food supply. After they had taken over they had merely erected walls around the cities and left the survivors to do as they would within these pens. Except, of course, for the thralls and the serum.

The thralls were not vampires, but not fully human either. The vampires could not function in the daylight, so they needed others to police their food supply. The thralls, so named due to their total bond of obedience to the vampires, had all been bitten but not fully drained. The condition gave them strength beyond human capabilities, but nowhere near the level of their vampire masters. They were allowed to live in luxury and do as they pleased with their charges, so long as the quota of fresh blood was achieved.

"God-damned serum," Harris fumed silently as he passed two thralls manhandling a woman too doped to defend herself.

The vampires had developed the serum to keep the humans docile. Each month everyone was forced to attend their local clinic for a fresh injection. The thralls kept records; they rounded up and killed anyone who failed to attend. They didn't know much about the serum or how it worked, but they did know that it acted to slow down the body's ability to interpret signals from the brain.

Each and every one of the people living in the city were fully aware of the horror around them, but were physically unable to do anything about it. Although the city was surrounded by walls, each person inhabited their own private cell: able to eat, dress and perform simple, mundane tasks, but completely incapable of acting independently.

Harris had grown up in this city and it tore his heart to see the once beautiful Town Square, always awash with blooming flowers and laughter, now desolate and dark. His father had brought him here regularly and they'd sit and watch the world go by, neither one saying anything as they soaked up the life that surrounded them. Harris felt deep regret when he remembered his parents. His mother had been the glue that held the family together, although he never knew how she had put up with three men in the family.

She had died of cancer two years previously. Soon after that his brother Josh had taken off and they hadn't heard from him since. His father, once a tall mountain of a man, had shrunk terribly after the stroke last year and, though the doctors had said that he should fully recover, he never had. Harris knew that no medicine could have treated the real reason for his death. His wife's passing had drained his vitality and spark; the prospect of a lonely old age was just not worth fighting for.

Harris had enrolled in the local university to study Engineering and, although he had plenty of friends, he often came down to the square alone for lunch to enjoy the area's sunshine and vitality and remember happier times. The fountain in the middle of the square, previously the centrepiece with water gushing from its twin spouts, was now dry. Clumps of weeds and dead flowers spilled out over the fountain basin.

He stopped at a red brick building at the end of the street and joined a queue of about ten people. When he finally shuffled into the serum room, he suppressed the urge to run, and had a difficult time concealing the look of shock that wanted to register on his face.

Twelve thralls, he thought frantically. He tried to keep his emotions under control. There had never been more than four before.

Harris' heart skipped a beat when two thralls approached him. The first grabbed his right arm roughly, while the other pulled up Harris' sleeve and plunged a large needle into the soft flesh just below the elbow. Pain shot through his arm and Harris bit down firmly. He clamped his teeth firmly together to stifle the scream that threatened to burst from his throat. Somehow he maintained the stoical look of indifference that he assumed this "test" was meant to challenge. Properly sedated humans would feel the pain, but be unable to react to it. Only when the thralls moved on to the person behind him did he allow a small grimace to appear.

Thoughts jumbled through his head. *Had they been discovered? Did the thralls know how they avoided the serum?* All the time that his mind frantically searched for an answer his body continued to shuffle along in the queue. His heart hammered in his chest, but he reasoned that the thralls couldn't know everything. If they did then they would have searched both arms much more closely. This test obviously meant the vampires knew that some humans had figured out a way to avoid the serum, but they didn't yet know how. These thoughts calmed Harris somewhat and he was still deep in thought when he reached the top of the queue.

At the end of the room the serum dispenser squatted on a low table like some huge, ugly bug. This was the time he was most vulnerable. Harris pulled up the sleeve of his left arm. As he plunged it into the small hole in the top of the machine, he turned it clockwise as far as he could. He prayed the guards would not notice which arm he used.

The machine was designed to inject the right arm with serum. The rebels normally coated their right forearms with a skin coloured sack that gave the impression they had received their usual dose. It wasn't an ideal solution, but a combination of luck and general apathy among the thralls had worked in their favour until now. Anticipating that the last attack would elicit some sort of check on that arm, they had switched the packs to the left instead. Aligning the left arm was quite awkward and, if they survived today's check, they would have to come up with another plan from now on.

The pressure relaxed. He withdrew his arm and started for the exit as quickly as he dared. Suddenly a hand gripped his shoulder and two thralls moved in front to block his path. He kept his face expressionless, but, in contrast, his mind frantically weighed the options. The thrall on his right grabbed his left arm and was about to raise the sleeve when a commotion began behind them.

A man had broken from the queue. In his haste to get to the exit he knocked two thralls over. Shouts and obscenities filled the small room and thralls seemed to come from everywhere at once to give chase. Harris nearly fainted with relief when the two guards who had stopped him turned and disappeared after the fugitive. Shots rang out and Harris cringed with every retort. Bullets flew after the man, but somehow the first volley missed him, tearing chunks out of the wall instead. Harris watched as the man reached the door, and he willed him on. For a minute it looked like he might make it, but then one of the thralls shouted in triumph.

The man jerked as a bullet ripped into his left shoulder. The force of the impact sent him sprawling to the floor and Harris saw his face for the first time. *Powell!* he thought. *My God he's only twenty years old.*

The thralls were on him in a second. They kicked and punched Powell viciously until finally he lay still and unmoving. Harris boiled inside, but had no choice but to continue his forward shuffle. He passed the thralls while they congratulated themselves and was sorely tempted to forget the pretence and run screaming into the middle of the group.

He ached to lash out and deliver some of the same punishment to these inhuman monsters, but the worthless gesture would only get him killed and dishonour Powell's sacrifice. Harris forced himself to look straight ahead and finally reached the door. He exited and, back out on the street, drew in a deep breath and exhaled it slowly.

He continued walking until he reached a small alley about two blocks from the clinic. He took his time to cautiously look around before he slipped out of sight. Once in the alley, his knees wobbled and he slumped against the wall. Harris retched and his body convulsed with the relief and frustration of the last hour.

"That was way too close," he muttered.

He remained there for some time and listened to his heartbeat thunder in his chest. Finally he pushed himself away from the wall and raised his sleeve. He peeled the flesh-coloured pack off his arm and smiled at the extra weight. He ripped a hole in the pack and watched the serum drain out and pool on the ground. After he finished he replaced the pack and left the alley.

CHAPTER
FOUR

"We're not ready!" Dan Harrington shouted. He slapped his hand on the table to emphasize the point.

"We'll never be ready at this rate," answered Harris. He rose from his chair and glared into Harrington's eyes. "We lost Powell today and damn near four others at the clinic. Once they examine Powell you can be sure those bloodsuckers will figure out how we're getting around the serum's effect." Harris sat back down wearily. "If we wait any longer, it'll be too late."

He looked around at the other members of the committee. Twelve people, seven men and five women, sat around a small table that occupied at least half the storeroom they used for their meetings. The group met once a week in an abandoned warehouse by the waterfront. The intention of these meetings was ostensibly to discuss survival strategies, though Harris was beginning to realise that the meetings had more to do with lonely, scared people wanting to be with others than any grand plan.

The room was murky; the only light they could afford was a cloaked lantern in the centre of the table whose pale light valiantly kept the darkness at bay. The cloying smell of fish and diesel oil hung heavily in the air.

Harris returned his gaze to Harrington. The stress of the last few weeks was beginning to show. Harris took the time to really look at him and, for the first time, noticed that the other man had lost quite a bit of weight. This once virulent, powerful man, the former CEO of a major corporation, seemed now to be shrinking. His shirt hung loosely on a frame that had once bulged with hard muscle. His steel grey hair, worn in a severe crew cut, had already begun to turn pure white. Harris could see the frustration in Harrington's face, and he worried about the older man's pasty complexion. Harrington had always been a tower of strength for their motley band of survivors, but the stress of such a responsibility was evident.

Bill Johnson sat at Harrington's right hand, as always. Johnson was thirty-five, mostly bald, and fervently loyal to Harrington. He was already half out of his seat, his face red with anger, when Harrington put a calming hand on his shoulder and motioned him to relax.

Lucy Irving, a matronly woman of indeterminable age, sat beside Johnson. Harris could see her shift her gaze between the two antagonists as if she were at a tennis match. Her hand lay poised over a half-filled page of the meeting's minutes, pen at the ready. *It's funny*, he thought, *no matter how circumstances changed people still gravitated to similar job roles in life.*

Scott and Bill Anderson came next in line. The twins shared the same easygoing attitude, a fact reflected in how they carried themselves and dressed. Their fresh faces, blue eyes and blond hair belied their sharp minds—until they spoke, that is. Then it became evident there was more to them than was evident at first.

To Harrington's left sat John Kelly, a wiry, un-likable man who could cause adverse emotions in a complete stranger within minutes of their first meeting without even trying. Next to him sat Sandra Harrington, strong-minded, independent and the daughter of "The Boss," as she referred to her father.

"He's right, you know." John Pritchard's response interrupted Harris' thoughts. "In light of today's debacle we have to assume they know about the arm padding. By the next Injection Day they'll either have caught us all or we'll be on the run. Either way we'll be dead inside a month.

Personally, I'd prefer to take a few out with me rather than end up as dinner."

A chorus of murmurs swept through the people gathered at the table.

"I agree with you, John," Harrington answered. The group leader wore a pained expression and his eyes were tired. "But it's not that simple. We're not talking about a small hit and run attack here and there. We'd have to take on the vampires at night and we've never done that before. Those bastards are fucking lethal at night. The thralls herded up most of you after the plague hit, but some of us held out for a few days in a police station outside of town. We managed to hold the thralls off for two days and felt pretty cocky until one of the vampires arrived."

Harrington paused, glanced around the table for emphasis, and then continued.

"It took five minutes for that bastard to demolish the building and take out twenty armed people. They move at awesome speeds and can lift a man with one hand. They can turn your mind inside out if you look at them, and these things are useless against them." He threw an automatic pistol on the table and the weapon's thud on the wood made everyone jump. "We can't go head-to-head with them. They're too strong."

Harrington had directed his last words, and his stare, at Harris. The younger man tried to hold the look, but then averted his eyes to glance around the table. He could see that Harrington had hit home and he was loosing this fight once again. He knew that most of the people around this table saw him as impotent, and these arguments had become something of a regular occurrence. He continually pushed for more raids, more risk, while Harrington would let him say his piece and then knock him down with the same arguments.

Harris had gained support with the younger committee members, but Harrington was very persuasive and had, up till now, always won. This time, though, Harris firmly believed that there wasn't going to be another meeting unless they did something drastic.

Harris made a decision and rose to his full height, steeled himself and began to speak. "I admit I have never seen the vampires in action up to now. I also know we may have little chance of success, but two hundred people are about to be slaughtered tomorrow night. This will be in direct retaliation for our raid yesterday and I just can't accept that."

"They will be killed anyway," Harrington interrupted. "You can't risk our entire group, and possibly the last of this planet's free people, on a matter of morality."

"Free?" Harris repeated sarcastically. "You don't call this existence free, do you? We're no freer than those other poor, drugged sods." He paused and looked around the table, meeting each person's eyes in turn. "In fact, we're worse off. We have the ability to do something about it and we're just sitting here. Maybe we should forget the patches and save the bastards the trouble of looking for us."

He looked over at Sandra and received a wink in return.

"Tomorrow night," he continued, "we have a chance to make a difference. My plan calls for surprise. Yes, we might fail, but think what success might mean. We total only twenty-four in number, and that took us six months to achieve. After tomorrow we could have two hundred more."

"With that number we can all leave the city and set up in the cave," John Pritchard added with a nod of encouragement to Harris.

"We have discussed that till we're blue in the face," interrupted Harrington wearily. "We can't survive out there. If we leave the city the vampires will know who we are and search till they find us. At least here we're anonymous."

"Not for much longer. How are we going to bypass the injections now? The only reason Sandra, John, Pat or myself are here now is because the thralls were too busy kicking the shit out of Powell to notice us."

Harrington looked down at the table and Harris felt the tide turning. This was the first time he had ever succeeded in making Harrington back down. Okay, reminding him that his own daughter was in that group this morning was a low blow, but there wasn't time to debate anymore.

"Dan, we have no choice." Harris lowered his voice as he leaned over the table. "If we win tomorrow, then we can really begin to hurt them."

"And if we fail?" Harrington asked with a raised eyebrow.

"If we fail," Harris repeated, "then at least we'll take as many of those fuckers with us as we can."

The two men stared at each other. Neither gave way. Then, slowly, a sad smile appeared on Harrington's face and he said, "I hope you're right."

CHAPTER
FIVE

T he moon shone brightly in an otherwise clear sky. Its light illuminated the surrounding area and forced Johnson and his two companions to retreat further behind the undergrowth.

"Bloody typical," Bill Anderson complained and received a withering look for his trouble.

The sound of shuffling feet reached them from further down the trail and Johnson risked lifting his head to get a better view. The trail led to one of the many guard compounds littered throughout the state. This particular one wasn't the closest to the city, but it was the nearest that could handle the number of humans involved in this particular punishment. Johnson sighed with relief when the group came into view. If they had chosen incorrectly, a lot of people would have died. As it was, he hoped that they wouldn't all die anyway.

About a hundred yards down the trail Johnson could see five thralls striding confidently toward them. The humans behind them were, in contrast, frightened and shuffled awkwardly along the trail. The line was orderly, with three abreast, and stretched as far back as he could see in the pale light.

"All right," he whispered as he turned to his companions. "When the guards go by we go. And for God's sake, remember to shuffle."

The first row of humans passed by and Johnson could see the look of pure terror in their eyes. *Goddamned serum*, he thought bitterly. Each and every human in that line was all too aware of what was about to happen, but was physically incapable of doing anything about it.

"Good, no vampires," he whispered and then the three companions slipped into the line and quickly fell into step with those around them.

Harris surveyed the scene below from his vantage point in a tree near the camp. A chain link fence reached some ten feet in height around the compound and culminated in a wicked spiral of barbed wire. The fence used to be electrified, but the guards had had it too easy for so long that they had become complacent. The fence had not been maintained in quite a while and current no longer flowed through it.

The overall shape of the compound was rectangular and measured some three hundred yards in length by two hundred wide. At each corner of the camp was a twenty-foot guard tower manned by at least one thrall. To his right Harris could see the barracks where the guards slept. Beside that was the motor pool, which housed some ten vehicles. Other buildings dotted the circumference of the camp. Harris could identify the armoury and mess hall easily enough, but the other buildings remained a mystery. To his left was the entrance to the compound, comprising of two huge gates flanked on each side by guard towers.

Harris shifted position. The pain in his stomach was from tension not cramp, so all he could do was ignore it while he watched the gates open. The guards led the doomed group into the camp and proceeded to assemble them in the large forecourt. When all the humans were assembled, a deathly silence descended on the camp.

Harris looked at his watch. *Three minutes*, he thought. In the distance he could hear the faint rustling noises they had all come to dread.

The noise grew louder and louder until, finally, Harris could make out the outline of the approaching swarm. They came from the east and their ebony darkness filled the sky.

They screeched and swooped at the assembled humans and added further to the terror of the pathetic group below. Each time they swooped into the compound the camp's lights illuminated their hellish features and Harris felt his resolve slip.

Twenty! My God, twenty of them, he thought in horror. *What have I gotten us into?*

One by one the creatures swooped down and began to change as soon as they touched the ground. Their wings shimmered and shrank; their heads began to flow as if made of jelly, and became flesh and bone. Their bodies filled out as their animal forms were replaced with a more human frame. The guards dropped to their knees in supplication and Harris gripped his radio tightly as the abomination before him strengthened his resolve.

"Group Two, begin," he whispered into the mouthpiece.

CHAPTER
SIX

"Group two, begin."

The words broke the reverie of the four companions. Harrington looked at each of his group. Sandra sat on his right. He had argued strenuously against his daughter coming tonight, but in the end it had been futile. John and Amy Stone sat to his left and held hands so tightly that their skin had long since turned white. He looked at each in turn. No words were spoken. None were needed. The group stood, embraced silently, and melted into the darkness.

John Kelly heard the radio crackle and knew that the time had long passed for changing their minds. They were committed. He always felt nervous just before an attack. His stomach would twist, his hands would shake uncontrollably, and pain would shoot through his body. Normally he would hide his nervousness and keep his hands in his pockets or sit alone and pretend to go over the plan one last time. Tonight, though, he was on his own. He could pace freely and count down the remaining seconds. He looked again at his watch and felt a calm come over him as all the tension passed.

It was time.

He bent down, picked up the axe from the grass and smiled when he saw that his hand no longer shook.

Harris waited until the guards on sentry passed his position and then dropped from the tree. They would take only five minutes to complete a full circuit of the complex, so he hurried over to the fence and began to climb. When he reached the top he threw a rubber mat over the barbed wire to protect himself. He looked around quickly to make sure he hadn't been seen and then pulled himself over and dropped to the ground. He checked his backpack was secure, pulled an Uzi machine pistol from its holster on his hip, and then disappeared into the darkness.

Sandra Harrington sighted along the aiming bubble at the end of the crossbow. The subject of her attention was a thrall in the east tower. She followed his pacing for a second and then allowed herself to exhale slowly. She forced herself to relax and said a quiet prayer. Her finger squeezed the trigger and she felt the weapon snap back against her shoulder. Many thoughts raced through her mind. Would her training pay off? Would she miss and cause the alarm to be raised?

The thrall suddenly jerked upright and then crumpled silently to the floor of the tower. Sandra smiled grimly and allowed the crossbow to swing from its strap. She looked again at her watch and then began to climb.

CHAPTER
SEVEN

"My Lord, the prisoners are all assembled as per your instructions." The captain of the guard rose from his knees and began his report. "The cameras will be ready in five minutes."

"Excellent," Nero replied and turned away to view the proceedings.

The cameras had been his idea. Screens had been set up everywhere and they would pipe the feed all over the city. He smiled at the thought of the terror this massacre would instill in the cattle. The serum might take away their ability to act independently, but it didn't stop them from being petrified. *Maybe this will make these rebels think twice before attacking their masters.*

Harris hurried through the darkness toward the motor pool. A line of jeeps and trucks were parked neatly in three lanes, and he ran through them to the fuel dump at the far end. He shook a number of cans and grunted in satisfaction when he found one almost full. Then he slipped back between the vehicles. He laid a trail behind him, removed petrol caps and sprinkled petrol liberally around the whole area. When he reached the last vehicle he poured the remaining fuel in a line leading back to the fuel dump.

When he was satisfied he checked around the grounds for sentries and sneered when he saw that most of them had given up their patrols to view the proceedings in the centre of the camp.

Morbid bastards, he thought, and then slipped silently toward the barracks.

Johnson could feel his heart thumping in his chest and sweat trickling down his face. He fought to remain still, but couldn't help pressing his left arm tighter against his side to ensure that the miniature crossbow was still strapped there. His eyes moved wildly from side to side while he took note of the each of the vampires' positions.

"Four minutes," Harris muttered to himself as he set the final timer and placed the charge in position under the barracks. Sweat rolled freely from every pore while the thralls moved about above him. At one point he could even see the wood of the floor dip dangerously close to his face when a guard stopped to warm himself against a radiator.

Harris thumbed the safety off his machine gun and rolled out from under the last of the five wooden structures along the western fence. He checked again for patrols and then made his way toward the assembled group in the forecourt.

The captain approached Nero and fell to his knees. "Camera uplink is now ready, my lord."

"Excellent," the vampire hissed and swept around to face his clan. "Come, let us show this rabble the price of resistance." And with that the vampires approached their terrified prey.

Johnson watched the vampires approach and slowly moved his hand toward his side. *God, I hope the others are in position*, he thought desperately, *or this is going to be one short-lived act of defiance.*

Just then a loud explosion shattered the silence. Four more quickly followed, so close together that Johnson thought it was one long thunder crack. He ripped the crossbow from its hiding place at his side and sent his first shot at the lead vampire.

Harrington heard the explosions and tried to blot out the scene of mayhem below him. All five of the buildings along the west fence had exploded and now burned fiercely. Thralls stumbled out of the ruined barracks covered in flames, screaming hideously as their flesh burned and crackled in the heat. An orange glow illuminated the camp. It undulated as the flames waxed and waned and gave the whole scene a surreal, hellish appearance.

The vampires recovered quickly. Harrington saw one of them grab the captain and shake him violently. Harrington couldn't hear what was said, but the vampire screamed at the thrall and gesticulated at the burning buildings. The captain seemed to recover and gathered some thralls to investigate. Harrington took all this in from his position in the west tower and then aimed his crossbow at his next target.

Bill Anderson saw his first shot bury itself in a vampire's chest. The creature howled and Anderson thought his ears would burst. Blood sprayed from the creature's chest. It flayed about and waved its arms in agony as it tried to remove the wooden quarrel. Men rushed to help the vampire, but the creature was so frenzied with pain that it lashed out and its razor sharp talons tore them apart. Some of the thralls screamed and fell to the ground holding bleeding limbs, while others backed away until, finally, the creature collapsed.

Anderson took aim at a second creature, but his eyes could not match the speed with which it moved. One minute it was 10 feet away and the next it had torn the crossbow from his grip. Anderson smelled the fetid breath and offered up a final prayer when, suddenly, the creature jerked upright and collapsed at his feet. Anderson stared unbelievably at the corpse and then noticed the quarrel. He looked up to see Sarah Harrington in the East tower and waved briefly, but she had already reloaded and moved on to her next target.

Anderson shook himself, looked around, and then dove to the ground as bullets shredded the air where he had stood.

He rolled to where his crossbow had fallen, reloaded and once again joined the fray.

Harris watched the chaos from the motor pool. Six vampires were dead and twenty or so thralls were either dead or injured. Quite a few of them had died in the confusion by their own masters' hands. He saw the captain of the guard gather up five thralls and approach the burning buildings. When they came level with his position, he lit the trail he had laid earlier and ducked low behind the vehicles to exit out the back of the motor pool.

Seconds later another round of explosions ripped through the night. One after another the explosions continued as cars and trucks were thrown high in the air with awesome force. The captain stopped his patrol, shocked by the unexpected blast. Within seconds shrapnel from the machinery flew outward and shredded them to pieces.

Johnson was having trouble picking out a target. The vampires were too fast. To complicate matters further the prisoners were trying to get to safety, but their drugged bodies were so slow that they only got in the way. He watched in horror as one of the creatures stopped and savagely ripped the throat of a helpless prisoner. Johnson shouted with rage and pulled the trigger on his crossbow. The quarrel caught the vampire in the chest and buried itself deep into its heart. The creature went down screaming, but Johnson had no time to gloat. Suddenly machineguns roared and bullets tore into the prisoners all around him. The thralls had recovered from their initial shock and, unlike Johnson and his colleagues, they didn't care who they hit with their fire.

Johnson dived for cover and cried out with pain as a bullet ripped into his shoulder. He cursed his luck—that made two bullets in as many days. All around him bodies danced grotesquely as bullets were pumped into the unfortunate prisoners. Johnson ignored the pain in his shoulder and groped for a grenade at his belt. He pulled the pin and threw it at the largest group of thralls. He didn't wait to see the result, but instead continued to pull grenades from his belt and throw them until all four explosives were gone.

When the rage had subsided he looked around and frowned at the silence that had descended. Most of the thralls were dead, their bodies mangled by the force of the explosions, but some still stood. Bullets ripped into the ground all around him, but there was no sound.

I've gone deaf, he thought, and looked about him, seeing people run, fall and die in total silence. Everything seemed to move much slower than normal.

And then everything went black. I've gone blind, he thought frantically. But then the darkness moved and he looked up to see a vampire looming over him. He felt the teeth bite deeply into his neck and rip the flesh. He felt the warmth of his own blood as it poured down his neck and chest, and then the creature moved to look him in the eye. The last thing Johnson saw was the creature's look of triumph freeze as he pulled the trigger for the last time and sent the bolt deep into its black heart.

"Ten of the clan dead!" Nero stared at the chaos around him. "And by mere mortals. Impossible." Then the realisation hit him. "The cameras! The cattle will see."

Bullets flew everywhere, but it was the wooden bolts that sent icy fingers of fear through him. He sent out a high-pitched scream, inaudible to human ears, and gathered the other vampires to him. He pointed at the towers around the compound and the group took to the air. Nero strode over to the camera, killing anyone in his way regardless of whether they were soldier or prisoner. The heady scent of blood filled the air and the lust pulled hard at him, enticing him to abandon all reason and gorge himself on those around him. But he knew that would be the way to death. First he had to deal with those humans in the towers. Then he could feed.

Once the camera had been destroyed he changed and took to the air.

Kelly felt his heart quicken when he saw the vampires change and take to the air. He gripped the axe tighter, raised it above his head and brought it down savagely to cut through the taught rope. The branch that had been held in place by the rope snapped back with ferocious force and sent a hail of sharpened stakes into the air toward the vampires.

Nero screamed in agony as a stake ripped through his left wing. The rest of the group was above him, and he saw the hail of stakes pass through them moments later. Four vampires dropped like stones ahead of him. Stakes covered their bodies and they changed as they fell to the ground. Three others staggered as they began to loose height and spiral downward. Nero himself began to falter as incredible pain shot through his own wound. The area around the injury stung savagely and he knew that the humans had used silver coating on the stakes. The wound would never truly heal and the pain would serve to remind him of his carelessness for eternity.

He looked up and saw the remaining members of the clan fly through to safety. He called to them to abort the attack on the towers. They were too few in number to continue here tonight. He took one more look below at the camp. Fires raged out of control and bodies littered the ground. From below, the sounds of cheering filled the night.

"Celebrate for now!" he said. "I misjudged you once. Next time I will be ready and I'll feed on your bones."

With that he looked for his companions and limped after them.

CHAPTER
EIGHT

T he compound resembled a scene from Dante's Inferno. Bodies littered the ground and moans filled the air as Harris walked through the carnage. The many fires that still burned throughout the camp illuminated the true horror of what had happened. In the centre of the camp he could see Sandra Harrington and Scott Anderson helping the survivors into waiting trucks.

"We all set?" Harris asked. He was shocked at how tired Sandra looked. Her face was drawn and her eyes had retreated deep into their sockets. The strain of the last few months had really taken their toll.

"These are the last," Sandra replied and smiled weakly. "Scott and I will travel with this lot and we'll meet up with John at the transfer point. We're due to meet Pritchard there. He and I will lead them to the Cave while the others dump the trucks."

Harris went over the plan in his mind and nodded. They had prepared their new home as best they could for the influx of guests and they were as ready as they would ever be. They had hoarded as much food and blankets as they could over the last few months. Water wouldn't be a problem due to an underground spring.

To call it a cave was a misconception. The facility was actually built half over and half underground. Pritchard had found the complex about 2 months before while scouting the area and they had planned for this day ever since. It consisted of a two-storey brick building above ground that stood within a walled enclosure on five acres. There were two more levels belowground, cut into the bedrock itself.

The Cave was situated ten miles from the city at the foot of a large hill and was surrounded by forest behind and to the east of the complex. A small river ran from the forest all along the west side of the complex, and a dirt road ran from the front of the building in a winding route to the main road. The rooms belowground were grey, lab-like and cold, and it was this that led the group to dub it the Cave. No one knew why it had been built, but it was generally assumed to have been military in nature.

"Okay, take care and watch for patrols. We can't let them find the Cave."

Sandra Harrington smiled. This time it reached her eyes and her whole face brightened. "Don't worry, we'll be careful," she said, and then touched his arm gently before she jumped into the back of the truck.

Harris watched until the vehicle disappeared from view and then turned back to the carnage.

"Harris!"

The shout exploded across the courtyard and shattered the relative silence in the enclosure. Harris snapped his head toward the sound and saw John Stone gesticulating madly by the armoury building. He broke into a run and, on arrival, was all but dragged around to the back of the building.

"Quick, follow me. You'll never believe what we found." Stone pulled Harris behind him and then suddenly stopped in front of the back door. He gestured for Harris to precede him into the building. Harris was amused, but he moved past Stone and entered the building only to stop dead in shock.

Lying on the ground in the middle of the room was a vampire.

Planks of wood and pieces of mortar surrounded the creature from where he had crashed through the roof. His body was pin-cushioned with stakes from the surprise aerial attack, but none had pierced his heart. Normally a vampire would be able to survive such an attack and walk, if not actually fly, away, but the group had long ago learned a few tricks when dealing with vampires. All the stakes were tipped with silver, which acted as a poison to the vampires. While it didn't kill them, it rendered the area around the wound immune to the vampires' virulent healing abilities. This resulted in a wound that never fully closed and caused constant pain.

This vampire, however, was going nowhere. Harris counted seven stakes from where he stood, and he could see the creature was in terrible pain. The vampire could barely move as the silver coursed through its body and fought and easily overcame its immune system, if the number of open and suppurating wounds on its body were any indication.

"Get a container and soak up as much of that blood as you can so we can test it later!" Harris shouted the order while his mind raced with the possibilities. "We might find something that'll kill these bastards without having to face them directly."

They had been trying for months to get fluids from the vampires but, once dead, the creatures tended to reduce to a sizzling goo that proved useless for analysis. Nobody in their right minds approached a vampire that was not dead, so this was the first chance they'd had to get a live creature's blood.

"What do we do with him when we get the sample?" Stone asked.

Harris looked up at the brightening sky. "Leave him to enjoy the sunrise."

Harris left the armoury building. Most of the group was gone and an eerie stillness hung heavily in the air.

"Come on, hurry up. We've got to go before those bastards get here."

The group's plan allowed for twenty minutes between the first shot and the first response from the nearest thrall base in the city. Seventeen minutes had already lapsed and it was past time to be gone. In the middle of the courtyard Harris saw a hunched figure he recognized as Dan Harrington. He walked over.

"Sandra got off ..." he began to say to ease her father's mind, but his voice faltered when he saw the body of Bill Johnson in the man's arms. In all the excitement Harris had forgotten about Johnson. He immediately felt a terrible guilt.

Harrington looked up at Harris. "Was it all worth it?"

Harris paused and knelt beside the body. "I think you know the answer to that," Harris replied. "We saved one hundred and seventy people tonight. I don't know about you, but that'll do me for an epitaph."

The two men locked eyes.

"We really must go. The first response team will be here any minute," Harris pressed gently.

He picked up a stake from the ground and handed it to Harrington. With a sigh Harrington placed the point of the stake over Johnson's heart and leaned heavily on it until the point pushed through the heart and into the soft earth below.

Harris looked up when he heard the first sounds of a helicopter in the distance. Both men stood and melted into the few remaining shadows of the surrounding forest.

The four trucks raced along the road. Jack Ryan drove the lead truck with wild abandonment and grimaced every time he missed a gear and the engine screamed in protest. His heart still beat like a jackhammer from his encounter with Nero. The master vampire had limped back to town and stormed into the thralls' barracks. Ryan had been there with his commander when the door literally burst open and flew across the room.

"What are you doing sitting on your arse?" Nero spat the words at the commander. "Didn't you see what happened?"

Nero had reached the commander's desk in two strides. He leaned over, grabbed the commander's shirt and lifted him clear over the desk with one hand.

Ryan had fallen off his chair when the door had burst open and he sat sprawled against the wall while the scene played out in front of him.

"My Lord," the commander stammered, "we have already sent the helicopter and I have a truck being readied at this very moment."

"One truck!" Nero snarled and then without warning he ripped the commander's head clean off.

Ryan shuddered as he remembered the scene. The master vampire had placed his hand on the commander's head in a patting motion, as if the information had placated him. Then suddenly the commander's head was in one of the vampire's hands and the limp torso in the other. He had thrown the body across the room and the next minute he was looming over Ryan.

"I want you to round up every thrall in this base, pack them into every truck you have and get up to that compound." The creature spoke calmly, even reasonably, but Ryan saw the threat in its eyes. "They can't have gone too far. Find them and you will be well rewarded. Fail and you will join your colleague."

Ryan had scrambled to his feet and ran from the office in a panic. He screamed orders at the startled thralls and, in less than five minutes, had assembled the convoy and set off for the camp.

When Ryan saw the compound gates up ahead, he relaxed and eased off the accelerator. Just then he heard a loud blast and the base of a tree to the side of the road exploded. The tree began to fall forward and Ryan swerved to avoid it. He wrenched the wheel hard to the right, but the truck had been going too fast, and its momentum carried it off the road. Ryan lost control when the front tire burst and the truck tumbled into the trees that edged the road.

The men in the back of the truck were thrown violently from side to side in a giant parody of a washing machine. Screams drowned out the other explosions as ten more trees along the route exploded and fell onto the road. Ryan had just enough time to scream before the first tree crashed down and split the truck in two.

The other trucks stopped when they saw the lead vehicle veer madly and shoot off the road. Men poured from the back of the vehicles and spread out to investigate. Suddenly, there were multiple explosions all around them. They froze, looked around in confusion at the sudden attack, and raised their guns to cover the forest as if they expected a horde of attackers to emerge. Instead, the forest itself seemed to loom closer toward them. Wood creaked and groaned in protest. Huge branches swayed dangerously above them before they began to fall. The trees decimated the entire area. Metal and flesh were crushed with equal contempt. Their screams were drowned out by the thunderous cacophony of trees crashing to the ground. The many broken branches that fanned out across the area impaled any thralls that were not crushed.

Five minutes after the first explosion the dust settled on the clearing. The four trucks were completely demolished and the mangled remains within would sicken even the strongest stomach. Of the thirty thralls that had been sent on the mission, two were still alive when night came and the vampires arrived at the scene. Their pitiful pleas stopped abruptly when the vampires ripped their throats out and then took to the air in search of the rebels.

CHAPTER
NINE

The murmur of many disparate conversations filled the air while each group huddled together and discussed their views animatedly. Harris looked around and noticed the differences between this and the meetings that had gone before. The "old group" were still there, except, of course, for Bill Johnson, but now they had a few new members.

Two weeks had passed since they rescued the group from the compound and, as the serum wore off, many of the former prisoners were actively participating in the running of their little community.

Two weeks, thought Harris. *Has it really been that long?*

They had been lucky to escape the aerial patrols and get everyone here safely and undetected. Since then there had been so many air and ground patrols that it had been impossible to do anything but sit tight and wait. Their food stocks had grown dangerously low and tempers were beginning to fray as nearly two hundred complete strangers bounced off the walls and each other.

If we spend much more time here, thought Harris, *we'll save the vampires the job and kill each other.*

It hadn't all been bad, though. There had been two real finds among the group they had saved—miracles, if you believed in such things. The first was Pat Smith, a chemist by trade. Harris had never met a more enthusiastic and ebullient person in his life. The man was forty-ish with a balding head and large cheekbones that gave him the appearance of a chipmunk. He was small in stature but had jumped at the opportunity to analyse the blood samples they had obtained.

The second find was Father Matthew Reilly. At over six feet in height, and with a voice like rumbling thunder, Reilly was a godsend.

When the people first came out of the serum's effects most were disoriented and frightened and immediately gravitated into groups. Over the last few days some of these groups decided they could run things more efficiently than the current committee. Many fights had broken out between the different groups that jostled for power. In fact, the Cave had been very close to civil war when Father Matthew Reilly had made his presence felt.

Vince Crockett, a retired army captain and leader of the strongest of these groups, had stepped into the main hall with five others, all of whom were armed. Guns were a part of life now, but no one ever carried weapons in the living quarters. Most people didn't realise what was happening at first and ignored the group. It wasn't until Crockett fired a burst into the ceiling that the reality hit home. The sound of the gunfire had the desired effect and the crowd in the main hall took them very seriously indeed. Crockett proceeded to outline his plan for how the community should be run, and the crowd grew in a steady stream as word spread.

Harrington arrived and, over the next hour, a debate raged between the Cave's more vocal inhabitants. Evidently, Crockett's group was not the only one dissatisfied with the current arrangements, and the arguments became more heated on all sides. The fact that Crockett was armed was forgotten and everyone dived in to debate his or her views. The noise level rose steadily until, finally, people were shouting at each other across the room.

Then one voice rang out with such volume and authority that all the groups were shocked into silence.

"Look at you!" Reilly had begun. He did not shout, yet his strong voice easily carried to every person in the hall. "In less than two weeks we have already turned a victory into a defeat. Who needs the vampires? We are quite capable of destroying what could be the last of humanity all by ourselves."

Most people suddenly found the floor to be of extreme interest. Few could find it in themselves to look their colleagues in the eyes.

"And you, Crockett, what are you going to do with those?" Reilly waved contemptuously at the weapons. "We have one chance left. Are we going to squander it on petty jealousy and power plays, or are we going to prove that we're worthy of that chance? God gave you all two ears and one mouth. Use them in that proportion. You know where to find me when you decide."

With that Father Reilly turned and walked out of the hall. The auditorium was deathly quiet. After a while the debate resumed tentatively. Crockett and his group laid down their weapons. Each side spoke in turn and began to listen to the other's views being expressed. From that debate had come a new committee that more fully represented the many viewpoints within their little community.

The present conversations wound down and Harris' quiet reflections ended when Dan Harrington rose and called this day's meeting to order.

"Friends," he began, "we have much to discuss, so let's get down to it. It's been two weeks since the raid. Harris, can you fill us in on what's been happening topside?"

Harris had been voted unanimously to head up external excursions because of the success of his previous outings. He felt a little nervous now that he had to speak with so many new faces around the table.

"Patrols have been pretty constant over the last few days. Thralls search during the day and vampires by night. They're throwing everything they have at it, blanketing whole sectors and searching everywhere. It's only a matter of time before they come here. One good thing, though, there does seem to be a window—we can move about during the two-hour period each side of dawn. The vampires tend to stay near their nests and the thralls start to become sloppy when their shift comes to an end. Bottom line is that if we have to go out in force and get back undetected, then we can, as long as we stick to the timetable."

"Thank you, Peter." Harrington looked over to Lucy Irvine. "Lucy, can you give us a state of the nation please?"

Lucy Irvine remained seated. Harris had always considered her a shy woman with people but had come to realise, as had many others, that where business was concerned she took things very seriously and had no problems defending her views. Her obvious flair for organisation and administration had made her the perfect choice for quartermaster and she ruled the allocation of supplies with a firm, but fair, hand. She fidgeted with a few files before her and then took a deep breath before she began.

"It's not that good, actually. We now have one hundred and eighty three people in the facility and have supplies for another two days."

"But I thought we had stocked up with enough food when..." John Kelly began to rise as he spoke.

"Mr. Kelly!" she snapped. "Would you please sit down and let me finish?"

The authority and force with which Lucy Irvine spoke surprised everyone in the room, and Kelly plopped back into his seat under her withering glare.

"As I was about to say," she continued, "we stored the stockpiled supplies in lab three on the second level. At that time, the room's temperature was perfect. Unfortunately, the room is next door to the generator. When we turned it on, the motor heated the walls and all the supplies stacked against the opposite side of the wall spoiled."

A low moan rippled around the table.

"We also have another problem. Two of the children have picked up an infection of some sort and their temperatures are dangerously high. Jill Ahern, most of you know her," heads nodded, "says that normally this could be treated easily with the correct medicines, but, in their absence, the infection could prove fatal. In such closed quarters, the chance that others have already contracted the same virus is high. We could be facing an epidemic."

The assembly was shocked. No one spoke for an uncomfortably long time. Finally, Dan Harrington rose.

"Well, the words 'shit creek' and 'paddle' come to mind." People laughed at his quip, a pressure valve that relieved the tension. "Captain, could you fill us in on how things are going on the home front?"

The appointment of Vince Crockett as Head of Defense was a surprise to many, but not to Harris. He knew how canny Harrington could be. Appointing Crockett placated the largest opposing group in the community. To be fair, though, Crockett was doing a great job.

Despite his takeover attempt, he was one of the few people in the community with actual military experience. It would have been criminal to waste him. The man's intolerance of those who failed to meet his standards disturbed Harris though, especially since most of the community fell far below those expectations. However, he did bring with him a wealth of knowledge and soon had everyone in the community, including the older children, training every day to improve fitness and familiarise themselves with firearms.

He had also shown a flair for strategy and had set up excellent defenses, something the original committee had sorely neglected. Once voted onto the committee, Crockett threw himself into his role with single-minded determination and had already created many particularly nasty surprises for any attacking force.

Glad he's on our side, Harris thought as the captain rose.

"As you all know, we're quite lucky in the location of this facility. Natural defenses like the forest and the river surround us on three sides, and I have plans for a few surprises there." Crockett grinned and Harris couldn't help but feel sorry for anyone trying to sneak up on them from those directions.

"However, we're rather exposed at the front. I've had small teams work on a few defenses there, but we have to scatter every time we hear a helicopter or see a land patrol. And any obvious changes to the landscape have to be camouflaged to prevent detection. As you can imagine, work is slow. I have asked that the house proper, that is the floors above ground, be used as little as possible. The building must appear abandoned when patrols come to investigate and drills should be run to keep noise to a minimum. Although the entrance to the underground facility is difficult to find, it would not go undetected in a concerted search.

"I would like more heavy weapons for the wall defenses," he continued, "but transporting them back here without leaving a trail is proving difficult, to say the least. Weapons training is progressing, but we can't afford to use live ammunition, so how effective people will be in an actual attack is still unknown. I would estimate that we have twenty people proficient in weapons. The rest are untried in a battle situation and could be beneficial or detrimental when faced with a real life-threatening situation. We won't know until it happens."

Crockett shrugged apologetically and retook his seat.

"Pat," Harrington next addressed the chemist, "have you any update on the blood sample?"

"Oh, yes, indeed," Smith responded. "It really is quite fascinating. I have not had much time so far, but things are proceeding quite well. The blood itself, although you can't really call it blood as such, is more like a parasitic suspension. The cells feed off the living organisms contained in our blood, but need to do this more often as the vampire's level of exertion increases. The two distinct cell types in the sample are completely different from human cells. I cannot identify them further with the current equipment, but obviously when a human undergoes the change into a vampire it happens at a DNA level. They truly are a separate species. I must admit I have no idea how they heal so quickly, but, interestingly, adding silver nitrate to the sample seems to hold some cells in stasis."

Smith noticed the questioning looks of his audience.

"Let me use an analogy. The silver acts like a sun cream. Although it lets fluids and some cells continue to flow, one type of cell is unable to move in the suspension, similar to the way sun cream allows certain tanning rays from the sun through and blocks the harmful ones. I'm guessing that this might be the regenerative cell and that is why silver-infected wounds do not heal.

"It puzzled me that we could shoot the creatures anywhere, including the heart, and they could regenerate, but a simple stake in the heart reduced them to goo. As an aside, the complete and amazingly fast breakdown of their bodies when they are staked happens because these cells I mentioned earlier, as well as being completely rewritten from the original human cells, also work at a hugely accelerated rate. This speed explains how they can heal so quickly—and why they break down so quickly.

"Anyway!" Smith paused briefly for a quick breath and continued again at his frantic pace. "I decided to investigate what was so different about wood. For years Old World cooks have maintained that the best platform for preparing food is wood. I haven't had time to investigate this in depth, but wood—once you clean it, of course—seems to have natural oils that ensure germs do not survive on the surface. I think this might explain why wood is so deadly to these creatures. The oil reacts against their accelerated systems."

"Would that not then apply if they got shot anywhere, not just the heart?" The question came from Crockett, who leaned so far forward that he was nearly on top of the table.

"Good question and one I pondered long and hard on," Smith replied. "Again, you'll have to excuse me, but the knowledge needed for a full analysis is far beyond me. I think that staking them in the heart concentrates the oil in the most vital area of the body, and the regenerative cells cannot work quickly enough. This accelerated battle to repair the heart causes an equally quick breakdown within the body. When the wood penetrates elsewhere in the body, then their healing ability has time to dilute the oil's concentration before it reaches the heart, and they survive. I have no idea why sunlight or holy water has such an effect. Scientifically, the sample should burn up when exposed to either, just as the vampires themselves do. I tested this and found that the sample remained completely unchanged when exposed to either one, or even both, elements. At the moment I'm stumped."

"Doctor." All heads turned to Father Reilly who leaned forward as he spoke. "Would you not consider the theory that while the creatures themselves are evil, and as such are susceptible to God's elements, the sample itself is not evil and so remains unaffected?"

"Father, at this stage I'll accept any theory, but theology is even further from my field of expertise than DNA research." Smith retook his seat.

Harris looked around at the members of the committee. The emotions showing on their faces ranged from stoical acceptance to shocked wonder and he wondered where they might go from here.

He turned to Harrington as the worthy began to speak. "Well, people, there you have it. Any suggestions?"

After a brief pause the members of the committee began to debate, slowly at first and then gaining momentum as ideas were proffered, discussed and decided upon over the remaining two hours that the meeting lasted.

At the end of the discussion there was no argument and even less choice. They would have to attack a major installation, on the enemies' home ground, to get the things they needed to survive.

CHAPTER TEN

"Peter!"

Harris turned at the sound of this name and saw Sandra Harrington trotting down the corridor. His face softened into a smile when he saw her. "Hello there, stranger," he said.

"Yes, it *has* been hectic for the last few days, especially with the children being sick." Her smile faded at the thought of the growing sick list. "Anyway, that shouldn't stop you from visiting me," she teased back.

"I make it a firm rule never to enter hospitals, even to visit such a pretty nurse."

They both smiled at that and moved to the side of the corridor as people jostled past.

"It sure is busy out here," Sandra said as she nodded towards the throng of people.

"Yeah, we're about ready to go. Hopefully we'll bring back something that'll help the kids."

Sandra's face grew serious. "Listen," she began, not sure how to proceed. "You take care out there. This is a major operation. We've never done anything on this scale before and …"

"We don't have a choice." Harris interrupted and took her hand in his. "But we've gone over the plan so often I could do this blind-folded."

"When you come back we'll have to make time for each other."

"Count on it," he replied and then folded her in his arms.

"Harris!" The shout came from the entrance bay to the underground facility where a group of people waited.

"I have to go," he whispered and then hugged her tightly once more before he broke the embrace. His lips softly caressed hers and then he turned and hurried to the waiting group.

They hadn't had much time to develop a relationship, but a spark existed there nonetheless, and both of them knew it. Sandra Harrington admonished herself when the tears began running down her face. She had not known Peter Harris for long, but already she couldn't imagine life without him. She watched him make his way down the corridor and follow his team out to the elevator. At the last moment he turned. His jaw was set so rigid she feared his teeth would crack. They stared at each other and she mouthed the words, "I love you." She saw him begin to reply, but then the door closed with a loud clunk.

Harris surveyed the city from an old building outside the walled area. *Feels like I've been in this situation before*, he thought. The wall that stretched before him ran out of sight in both directions. Floodlights, perched every thirty feet or so, illuminated the surrounding areas. Thralls patrolled the ramparts and their posture and occasional stretching revealed their obvious boredom. Harris could see eight thralls from where he stood, but was certain that many more were inside the city.

When they left the Cave the group had split into three separate units to reduce the risk of being spotted. Each unit followed a pre-determined and totally separate route to the city. They had left an hour before dawn and it had taken his unit twenty minutes on a forced march to get into position. He had no way to be sure that each group had reached their positions because they had decided against the use of their radios this close to the city.

This was by far the biggest undertaking they had ever embarked upon. Thirty-five people were positioned around the city and another twenty people would leave the Cave soon with transport for the return journey. They had had a few scares on the way when they spotted patrols, but, luckily, the thralls were merely going through the motions and the vampires were more interested in returning to their lairs this close to dawn.

The committee had decided on three separate objectives for this attack. Group Alpha would make their way to the Hospital and scavenge anything useful there. This was considered a soft target because it had been abandoned since the vampires had taken over and the group consisted of only five people. Their main problem would be the mile long journey they had to make deep into thrall territory.

The Anderson brothers, Bill and Scott, led this group. John Pritchard would also accompany them. Harris hated taking three of his best men away from the assault, especially since they all had experience fighting the vampires. But they really needed medical supplies and the distance involved warranted the high calibre of men. Jenny White, one of their nurses and another very expensive resource, was with the group to ensure that only usable medicines and equipment were brought back. John Hackett completed the group. Harris didn't really know anything about the man other than he had been a farmer, but at six-foot-three and built like a linebacker, he reckoned that he'd be good for carrying if nothing else.

Group Bravo consisted of twenty people and they had the most critical mission of the three, namely food and general supplies. Unfortunately for the group, the thralls controlled the only consumable supplies left in the city and these were kept in their many barracks dotted throughout the city. Tonight's target was chosen due to its proximity to the city walls, but as luck would have it, this was also one of the largest occupied facilities in the city. Dan Reiss was leading the group in, and, in Harris' opinion, a better choice couldn't be found. As an original core group member, Reiss had the most experience of any of them. His group was made up of volunteers who had distinguished themselves during the many practice sessions they had run.

I hope to God this doesn't backfire on us, Harris thought, *the Cave will be virtually defenseless if we fail here tonight.*

Harris led the third group, Group Nero. He smiled at the name that defied the naming convention of the other groups. Harris' target was Nero himself. This was a big risk, but if they could destroy the city's head vampire, the ensuing confusion would give the group more time to establish themselves while the other vampires fought over the vacant leadership. They had identified the building Nero used as a base some time ago, but had never dared to attempt an assault before.

The three attacks were spaced out over a distance of some three hundred yards along the wall. They hoped that using multiple entry points would create more confusion and force the thralls to spread their forces over a larger area. Although Harris had successfully planned a number of raids so far, he still based his strategies more on his knowledge of historical battles and a lifetime of playing and designing war games than on any actual experience. In fact, before the vampires had taken over, the closest he ever got to real action was a few games of paintball with friends in the woods.

He hated planning other people's lives. It petrified him to think that people lived or died on the strength of his decisions. These weren't computer-generated pixels that could be renewed from a saved game. These were real people. If he messed up, people died. That was a hell of a responsibility and he had spent an hour with Father Reilly before they had set out. He explained his doubts and confessed his fears of the task that had been set for him.

Reilly had listened and asked him a question every now and then. Finally, he took Harris' hands in his and asked, "If not you, then who else? Is there anyone else in the community who could do a better job?"

Harris had studied all the new recruits over the last few weeks in the hopes that someone would be more suited to take on the responsibility. He thought that Crockett would be perfect, but Harrington had been firm that they needed both of them in separate roles if they were to survive; one for offence and the other for defense. Of all the others Harris had found no one. "No," he had replied.

"Then the responsibility is yours for now. Accept it and it will be easier to bear. People may die, but you have saved far more up to now than you have lost."

Harris shook himself from his reverie and looked at his watch. He counted down the last few seconds and then left his position on the roof to join his group. Timing was critical. They had to be gone before full light in order for the remaining darkness to cover their retreat. They were counting on the early hour and the suddenness of the attack to leave the thralls disoriented long enough to get the groups close enough to their base so they could abandon their vehicles.

The final seconds passed and then three large explosions rocked the night and everything went to hell.

Dan Reiss crouched near the wall and watched three team members plant the explosives. He kept a nervous eye on the thrall who paced along the rampart some ten feet above them and breathed a sigh of relief when the three men finished and retreated a safe distance.

"Two minutes to go," Reiss whispered to the men around him.

His heart hammered in his chest and his hands itched with sweat. This was the fourth raid he had been involved in, but this one was different. Up till now they had always had the element of surprise on their side. After the last attack, though, the thralls had doubled the number of guards on all of their installations. The people around him, many of whom he didn't even know, remained hidden from the thralls behind whatever cover they could find and he shifted position nervously. One good thing about the way the city and its environs had been left to deteriorate was the number of abandoned cars they could use as cover off the main traveled routes out of the city.

Reiss was a mechanic by trade, but had been a sergeant in the local reserve on weekends for the last ten years. His steel grey hair was cut short and his body was well muscled from years of physical training. This "experience" had earned him a command and he was terrified, not only at his own lack of real experience, but also because the men he led were a mixture of office workers, shop owners and factory employees.

Christ! he thought, *we even have a male stripper. What's he going to do, throw his thong at the vampires?*

Despite the tense situation he smiled and looked down at his watch once more. "Okay people," he whispered. "Get ready."

Philip Warkowski wiped his brow and brought the rifle's telescopic lens back to eye level. He sighted on a patrolling thrall and followed him to the end of his allotted area. Warkowski had chosen his position well and from this rooftop he could see all of his targets without the need to change building. After he had dispatched his targets, his orders were to stay put and cover the retreat. Warkowski, however, had other plans.

He had been among the group that had been saved at the compound. He was deeply indebted to this group of rebels and had the highest respect for them, but when the thralls had taken him for their planned massacre, they had left behind his wife and nine-year-old daughter. The thought of them still in the city and at the mercy of the thralls consumed him.

He had pleaded that he be allowed to find his family and bring them out during the attack, but had been refused. If he was honest with himself he couldn't blame Harris for saying no. But that wouldn't stop him. Their house wasn't far from here and he planned to sneak by the main hotspots, find his family and return to his position with no one the wiser. His stomach knotted with worry, both for his family and because he felt guilty for leaving his post, but he reasoned that he really didn't have a choice. He glanced at his watch one more time and settled himself to the task in hand.

Scott Anderson and his team were the furthest along the wall in the least populated sector of the three designated target areas. He glanced at his people and marveled at their calm. His small group was comprised of a nurse, a farmer, a solicitor and two tech heads.

Hardly what you'd call an elite strike force, he thought, but the looks of determination on each of their faces gave him strength.

"Thirty seconds!" he whispered.

CHAPTER
ELEVEN

T he explosions went off simultaneously and tore large gaping holes in the wall. Bricks and mortar flew in every direction at fantastic speeds, and the flying shrapnel tore some of the thralls to pieces. Before the others could react, smaller cracks of gunfire broke out and added to the cacophony. All along the wall the thralls who had escaped the initial violence of the blast were dropped with well placed sniper fire before the assassins turned their deadly attention to the floodlights.

When the last of the lights went out, the three groups invaded the city.

Harris ran, climbing over the rubble, and sent a sustained burst of fire at two thralls who came running from a nearby guardhouse. Their bodies staggered as the bullets ripped into them, and Harris was already past them before they fell to the ground. The rest of Group Nero followed close behind and fired at anything that moved. Four thralls ran from a building in various stages of dress. Harris pulled a grenade from his belt and threw it at the group. The explosion flung their bodies into the air and the bloodied remains crumpled to the ground. Harris ran up the steps of the building and crashed through the door.

Three more thralls appeared. They were still groggy from sleep and Harris sent a hail of bullets into their midst. He heard a sound, whirled to his left and froze. In the corner he saw four women huddled together, their eyes petrified. He saw their naked bodies and kicked one of the corpses in disgust as realisation of their plight sunk in.

"Bastards!" he spat at the body nearest him and approached the cowering figures. He pulled a blanket from a nearby bed and gently laid it around the drugged women. "Henshaw!" he shouted as the worthy came through the door, "get these women dressed and take them out to the rendezvous point."

"But, sir, we don't have the time."

"I think they've earned a little compassion, don't you? Get them out. Leave them with one of the snipers and follow us to the target."

With that Harris stormed out of the house and vented his anger as he slammed another magazine into his weapon.

Group Bravo was pinned down just inside the city wall. Dan Reiss and his team had stormed through the breach in the wall only to be met by a hail of gunfire. Reiss dove to the ground and bullets passed only inches above him. He hit the ground hard and rolled, coming up in a crouch behind a large piece of the destroyed wall. Four of his team were not quite as quick and bullets decimated them. Five others had made it into the city and now lay behind whatever cover they could find.

The rest of Reiss' force was still on the wrong side of the wall.

He sneaked a glance around the wall. Six thralls with a heavy machine gun were dug in behind sandbags about thirty meters away.

"Shit!" he shouted and dodged back behind cover an instant before bullets rammed into the stone. "Just our luck. We would have to blow a fucking hole in the wall right beside an entrenchment, wouldn't we?"

The sound of the machine gun fire stopped and Reiss risked another quick look. The thrall controlling the heavy machine gun lay slumped over his weapon and two of the others were frantically trying to pull him away. Suddenly he heard a high-pitched crack and a second thrall fell facedown, the back of his head completely destroyed.

"Warkowski, you big, beautiful bastard!" he shouted when he realised what had happened. He signalled the other five members of his team and then broke cover and sent a deadly suppressing fire into the remaining thralls. Caught completely unaware by the turn of events, the thralls died without firing another shot.

"Come on quick!" he shouted to the rest of his force and they climbed over the rubble to advance on the main barracks. Reiss looked back to the building where he knew Warkowski was set up and, even though he couldn't see the sniper, waved his thanks.

Warkowski saw the figure wave through his scope. "You're welcome," he muttered.

He scanned the area surrounding the breach. Confidant that he had cleaned out all the thralls in his designated area, he laid down the rifle and prepared to enter the city.

Scott Anderson led his small group over the rubble of the destroyed wall. The section they had chosen to enter was dark and deserted. They had purposely come in through the docks because no one had used the waterfront area for two years now since the plague began. The hospital was situated about one mile to the West and Anderson could hear the gunfire and screams of the other two groups to the East.

"Poor bastards," he sighed and then slipped through the darkness.

CHAPTER
TWELVE

The thralls were using an old police building as their base of operations. The sheer size of the three-storey building was intimidating. It seemed to loom over Reiss and his men. The building overlooked a small square in front and smaller, one-storey buildings abutted it to either side. All the windows had bars on them and Reiss could see figures behind the frames as well as on the roof.

The square was completely clear of any debris, and the two hundred yards between their current position and the building was the perfect killing ground.

"Jenkins!" shouted Reiss. "Go round the back and cause enough of a diversion to take some of the heat off. Rodgers; see if you can find anything we can use in that entrenchment we passed."

Reiss risked a quick glance around the corner and recoiled violently as dust and debris flew into his eyes when bullets slammed into the wall. "Shit," he muttered, looking up at the sky, "only another ten minutes till dawn. We're running out of time."

Just then he heard a whoosh behind him, followed by a loud explosion, and finally a rebel yell. He looked around the corner again and this time the door to the building was in pieces. In fact, plaster and metal littered the entire area in front of the door.

"Look what I found!" The excited yelp came from a still grinning Rodgers who knelt to Reiss' left and held a smoking bazooka.

"Quick everyone!" Reiss shouted. "Let's get in there before they recover."

The men ran from their various hiding places and swarmed the building. The thralls recovered quickly, however, and bullets rained down from the windows and rooftop entrenchments. Men scattered under the assault. Reiss heard two more of his men scream and watched them fall to the ground. Anger blinded Reiss; he crashed against what was left of the door supports and threw a grenade inside. He waited impatiently for the explosion and then dove through before the dust had time to settle.

The interior was dark. Dust from the explosion filled the air and he could hear intermittent coughing as more of his men entered the foyer.

"Spread out!" he ordered. "Rodgers, take three men and clear out upstairs. Perkins, check out that door at the back. The rest of you, come with me."

Reiss was headed for the basement stairs when he heard a strangled cry behind him. He whirled in time to see a dark figure appear from the alcove, holding Perkins by the neck. The figure held the struggling man three feet off the ground by only one hand. Reiss blanched.

He looked out at the night sky and saw the first tentative rays of dawn appear over the horizon. *Shit*, he thought, *at least another five minutes before the bastard's in any danger. Christ, he could kill all of us and be back in his coffin in plenty of time."*

The sharp snap focused everyone's attention on the figure; Perkins ceased struggling and went limp. The creature threw the body across the room indifferently, with sheer, awesome power. The men watched in shock as the body crashed through a boarded-up window and hung limply over the windowsill.

Then the vampire disappeared.

Reiss heard a cry behind him and turned to see the creature attacking Jack Walton.

Fuck, he's fast, Reiss thought. But before the thought was completed, another of his team flew across the room like a rag doll and crashed heavily against the wall.

He's playing with us! Reiss glanced up again at the brightening sky.

Three men remained standing. Reiss looked around frantically for something to shoot at. Then the man to his left simply disappeared as if the floor had swallowed him whole. Reiss ran straight at the only other figure left standing. Just before he reached the man, a dark shape suddenly appeared between them. He got a quick impression of a pale face and impossibly long teeth, and then he felt the impact.

Reiss crashed into the vampire. Both of them went reeling across the room and hit the wall hard. Reiss felt the wind driven from his lungs. He slid to the ground and lay gasping on all fours. His chest hurt where he had collided with the vampire and he forced himself to take small breaths to ease the pain. Dust filled the air and Reiss cried out when the chalky dryness forced him to cough. Fresh pain racked his body, but it served to focus his mind. He remembered the vampire and looked up quickly. The creature was impaled on the remains of the boards covering the window where Perkins' body still lay over the sill. The creature merely smiled, despite the multiple punctures.

Reiss watched in terror while the creature pulled itself away from the wooden shards. Suddenly it stopped, shuddered, and then howled as a large hole appeared through its upper body. The hole expanded and blood poured from the wound in torrents. Reiss watched as more holes began to appear until the whole body came apart and literally melted in front of him.

"What the hell?" Reiss exclaimed. His mind raced, and then the first tendrils of sunlight pushed against the shadows around the window and crept into the room.

Of course, he thought, *sunrise, and not a minute too soon.*

Reiss looked around and sighed in relief when some of his men began to rise from where they had fallen.

"Thank God he was playing with us, eh?" The question came from Rodgers, who was the only man who hadn't been attacked. Reiss looked over at the young man. He was tall, that was the first thing anyone noticed about Rodgers, that and his idiotic grin. Reiss considered himself a good height at 6-foot-2, but he had to look up to this kid. *He couldn't be more than twenty-five,* Reiss thought, and had to smile himself when he saw Rodgers break into another wide grin.

"Can I ask you a question?" Rodgers asked.

"Go ahead."

"How did you know he'd go for me next?"

"I didn't."

Just then the door to the basement burst open and thralls poured in.

Bullets flew everywhere and both sides dove for cover. Rodgers staggered back, clutching his left arm, and collapsed against the stairs. Reiss felt a bullet fly past his cheek and brought up his own weapon. He fired a sustained burst into the thralls and ran for cover. Two of the guards were caught in the hail and they pirouetted wildly with each impact.

"Shit!" Reiss looked at his watch again. The two-hour window restriction and the threat of reinforcements made the timing of this whole operation very tight. The nearest barracks of any size was twenty miles across town and they had factored in a twenty-five-minute response time.

That left only ten more minutes.

CHAPTER
THIRTEEN

S cott Anderson and his group kept to the shadows while they ran through the city. The area was completely deserted, but they could see an occasional building with lights on and decided that they'd play it safe. The sounds of fighting still raged behind them, and they had seen at least one patrol on their way to the battle. Their group was too small to successfully carry out an ambush, so they could only hide and watch helplessly while the patrol passed by.

They came to the hospital grounds shortly after that and entered over the wall to the east of the building. Scott led his group across the overgrown grounds to the main wing. The night was still full dark and dawn was some fifteen minutes away when he saw the glow of a cigarette by the door. He jumped to the ground and tackled his brother, who hadn't seen the sentry. Both of the men hit the grass hard.

"What?" Bill began, but stopped immediately when he saw his brother motion for silence and point to the hospital entrance. Two thralls stood in front of the main door.

"Oh shit," Bill whispered. "Not as abandoned as we'd hoped."

"There must be something mighty important in there for them to have stayed with that racket going on back there." Pritchard indicated the sounds of fighting behind them.

Scott nodded his agreement. "We'll have to find another way in."

The sound of breaking glass seemed to fill the night. Each of the small group cringed at the noise.

"Careful," Scott Anderson looked balefully at his brother.

"Do you want to take over?" Bill looked indignant, but he continued to remove the sharp fragments from the window frame. The two brothers were famous for their quick tempers, but everyone knew that the constant sparks that flew between them were purely cosmetic.

The group had spent the last ten minutes looking for an alternative entrance, but the building had proved to be more of a fortress than a hospital. Finally, they had come across a small window set below ground level, the only window that didn't have light coming from within. They had to dig a small trench around the area just to get at it.

"Not what you'd expect from an abandoned hospital is it?" Pritchard asked. "We'll have to hurry; the sun is starting to come up."

Both brothers turned and gave Pritchard a withering look.

"Okay, I was just reminding you." Pritchard said defensively.

Finally Bill finished and pulled himself through the narrow opening and into the room. The rest of the group waited nervously outside, all of them riveted on the small, dark opening. After what seemed an eternity, Bill Anderson's face appeared and he motioned for them to follow. The tiny room barely held the whole group. Scott was last in and immediately joined the others by the door.

"Locked!" Bill Anderson spat out the word like a curse.

"Of course," Scott sighed. "This night just gets better and better. Next we'll find half the vampires in the city on the other side of the door."

"Don't tempt fate," warned Hackett as he bent down and fiddled with the lock. The tool he was using on the lock looked tiny in the grip of his huge hands. There was a muffled clunk and Hackett stood up. He looked sheepish when he noticed the others staring at him. "Result of a rather colourful youth, I'm afraid."

Scott smiled and opened the door just far enough to look into the corridor. "Well, at least the vampires didn't turn up," he said before he opened the door fully and stepped out.

"Not yet, you mean," Bill answered gloomily and followed him out.

"What are we looking for?" John Pritchard asked when the group had reached the end of the corridor.

Scott was about to respond when Jenny White interrupted.

"We used to keep the supplies in the basement before the vampires took over, so let's start there," she said and moved to take the lead. This was the first time she had made her presence felt within the group and Scott assumed that the familiar surroundings of the wards gave her confidence. The corridor was dimly lit by the first rays of the new dawn coming in through the window behind them. Scott felt very exposed in the open area and kept glancing around.

They passed many rooms, all of which were closed and locked. Scott paused to look through the glass partition of a few of the doors, but could see nothing other than empty beds stretching back into the darkness.

"This is getting weird," he thought. "Why clean up and lock all the rooms? Why are there guards out front?"

Every other building not used by the thralls had been left to deteriorate; even the ones where people still lived were slums. The serum ensured that the populace was kept in line, but it also ensured that people did not even have enough free will to make their surroundings comfortable. Scott shook himself back to reality and hurried after the group.

They reached a door emblazoned with a sign that depicted a stairwell. When they entered, they had to stop briefly and wait for their eyes to adjust to the darkness.

"Damn!" said Scott Anderson. "We have to hurry. We're due back at the wall in twenty minutes and we haven't found so much as a condom yet." He retook the lead and proceeded down the stairs. The enclosed space and the lack of light weighed heavily on the group. The short distance to the basement seemed to take an inordinate amount of time, but, finally, Scott felt the door handle and gripped it as a drowning man would a lifeline. He turned the handle slowly and opened the door.

The basement was illuminated so brightly that he was totally blinded when he opened the door. Spots swam in his vision and he closed the door rapidly, then waited until his eyes recovered.

"There's someone down here," he whispered. "There are more lights on down here than in Times Square."

The group readied their weapons and opened the door slightly. They let their eyes grow accustomed to the light and then slipped into the corridor.

The door opened out onto a long corridor. To the left it continued on for another two hundred yards, with many rooms dotted along the length, and culminated in a dead end. All the doors were closed and dark. To the right there were double swing doors and, through these, a large open plan room. The swing doors had small, in-built glass partitions, just like the wards. Scott Anderson crouched just below the partitions and peaked inside.

He could see two men in white coats. One was bent over a machine and the top of his bald head shone brightly in the fluorescent lighting. The second sat at a desk, writing. Scott pushed the door open with the barrel of his machine gun and checked out the rest of the room.

The room's stark, neat efficiency was in total contrast to the rest of the city. The work surfaces were clear, except for neatly ordered rows of phials and bottles. In the far corner there was a large collection of cardboard boxes. Anderson leaned in further and caught a glimpse of three more people busily filling the boxes with bottles. The workers were obviously drugged. They shuffled from the boxes to the table where the bottles were stored.

The serum! The thought leapt into Scott's mind. *Of course! That explains the security on the door. This is where they make it. We've hit the mother load.* Without further delay Anderson motioned the others to follow and entered the room. "Okay, move away from the desks and put your hands behind your heads."

The loud voice startled the men in the white coats. They froze like deer caught in a car's headlights and stared at the armed group that entered the room. Scott moved toward the men and the other four spread out to look for supplies they could use.

John Pritchard approached the three workers who stood rigid with fear and tried to calm them. Jenny White raced around the room and pulled boxes and bottles into a bag, yelping with pleasure when she recognised certain items. Scott moved across to the cardboard boxes and looked down at the large, litre-sized bottles. The green liquid even looked evil. That was the only way he could describe it—evil.

"This bottle contains the single most devastating weapon against humanity," he said.

By the time the humans had accepted the real threat of the vampires, the creatures had controlled half the country. They were, and still remained, a stealth creature. The vampires were devastating at night; they cleaved their way through flesh and armour with wild abandon. Bullets and grenades proved useless against their ever-increasing numbers. The military wasn't prepared for such an enemy and lost ground easily to the ravaging horde. However, the acceptance of this threat, along with increasing public knowledge, finally began to hurt the vampires. A new type of war emerged: one of pitched battles with huge numbers on either side, and the humans had the advantage of a full twenty-four-hour day. The fact that the vampires were completely defenseless during the day had really begun to hurt them. Any advances they made were quickly lost during the day when they had to retreat to darkened sanctuaries. Even the introduction of thralls only slowed down the inevitable and the humans had slowly begun to claw back their territory.

That was, of course, before the serum.

The vampires had introduced the serum into the food chain, infecting livestock, food processing and water sources across the world. The humans never knew what hit them. In the space of a week the battle was over. Humans lost the ability to defend themselves and the vampires simply walled off the cities and carved up the territory between the different clans.

The world as we knew it ended and it was all because of the contents of this bottle. The thought burned inside of him, the anger grew until he couldn't hold it in any longer. "How can you help them?" he shouted the question and crossed to where the two white-coated men stood. "Answer me!" he shouted and lashed out at the bald man. He forgot that he held the machinegun in his hands and Scott hit the man hard in the forehead with the barrel. The man flew backward and crashed into the boxes in the corner. Bottles smashed and the man cried out as broken glass pierced his skin. Still enraged Scott turned on the other man who cowered in the corner. He raised the weapon again.

"Easy," his brother's voice cut through the haze and Scott slowly lowered the weapon. "They're not worth it. Let's get what we came for and get out before someone comes."

"I'm afraid it's way too late for that."

The voice came from the doorway and everyone turned just in time to see the thralls enter the room.

CHAPTER
FOURTEEN

"Is that it?" Henshaw asked. He nodded toward the small townhouse at the end of the street.

The area they were in had been an exclusive part of the city once. Set some three miles from what had been the city centre, the area boasted cute, three-storey houses dotted along a tree-lined manicured green, the perfect, relaxing environment to go home to after a hard day's work.

"Yeah," answered Harris. Henshaw could see that Harris wasn't himself. It had taken fifteen minutes to get here since the initial assault and Harris hadn't spoken once.

Group Nero, spread out across the green, used the trees for cover. The darkness was still dense enough to cover their approach, but the first tendrils of dawn were already beginning to make their presence felt on the horizon. Three thralls patrolled outside Nero's lair.

"What's the plan?" Henshaw turned to Harris.

"Plan?" Harris looked blankly at Henshaw.

"Are we going to hit front and back in a coordinated attack or …"

"Nope," interrupted Harris.

"Then how are we going to get in?"

"We go straight through the front door, of course." With that Harris rose and strode purposefully toward the house. He reached behind him and brought his machinegun to bear and let loose a sustained hail of bullets.

"Harris!" Henshaw shouted. "Wait you can't…oh, shit!" He turned to the other team members. "Come on, we're committed now. Let's help the crazy son of a bitch."

Harris burned with rage. The gun in his hands jerked violently and a constant stream of bullets ripped into the three thralls in front of the house. Their bodies flailed wildly with each impact, and Harris merely walked over the corpses while he reloaded and then kicked the front door in.

"Harris!" Henshaw shouted and grabbed him back just as bullets ripped through the air where Harris had stood. "Harris!" he shouted again, this time looking him in the eyes. "Getting killed isn't going to help." He held Harris tightly in place despite his struggling. "Snap out of it."

Harris stared into Henshaw's eyes and slowly the bloodlust receded. Bizarrely, he could see a reflection of his own features in Henshaw's eyes. The visage reflecting back at him shocked him so much that he stopped struggling. His face was pale, bloodless even. The lack of colour was further exacerbated by the blackness of his hair which hung limp and heavy with sweat.

Is that really me? He thought as he stared at the reflection. He shook himself and blinked at Henshaw as if awakening from a dream. "Okay," he whispered, "I can manage from here."

The sounds of gunfire continued to reverberate around the two men. More team members joined them by the door to shelter from the fire that rained down from the upper storey.

Two of the team lay on the street, blood pooling around their still bodies.

My fault, Harris thought. The rage still burned within him, but this time he would control it and use it to his advantage. He took two grenades from his clip, pulled the pins and lobbed both through the open door. The explosions rocked the entire building. Masonry and debris flew out on to the street.

"Ashley, Kelly, you stay here and watch our backs. The rest of you follow me."

The scene that met them when they entered was one of total destruction. The spacious hall they entered led to an open living area and kitchen. Furniture lay strewn about and the bodies of three thralls lay limp and bleeding over the broken remains.

"You know the drill, guys," Harris ordered as he walked through the house. "Check the bodies, make sure they're dead. Clean out any others. Three upstairs, four down here, and the rest of you find that bastard's coffin."

"Are you sure he's here?"

"He was last night. Most of the clan set up in large houses with their own grounds. The thralls patrol during the day, and that's what made it so easy to track them. Nero, however, is clever. He set up in an ordinary house where no one would expect to look. It took us months to find him and we only stumbled on this place by pure accident." Harris spoke while he walked through the house and tapped the walls to check for a basement or false panel.

Suddenly terrible screams came from upstairs. Gunfire erupted and then, just as suddenly, there was silence. Henshaw started to run for the stairs.

"Wait!" Harris warned. He crossed to the door and looked out at the sky. "It can't be a vampire," he stated when he saw the bright sky. "Okay, let's do this in relays of twos. We're good for ten minutes before we have to pull out."

With that Harris and Henshaw started up the stairs.

Once they reached the top of the first landing the next team leapfrogged past and entered the first room.

"Clear!" came the shout from within and the next team kicked in the door of the second room. They continued until all of the rooms had been searched.

"Okay, next floor," Harris ordered.

A dark shape suddenly appeared on the top landing. Harris caught an impression of fur and teeth and a smell of decay, and then the shape launched itself down the stairs. It crashed into Parsons, who had been halfway up the final stairs, and the two bodies tumbled down to the landing. In the small second floor area the group were tightly packed together when the struggling pair came crashing among them. Bodies flew everywhere like pins in a bowling alley and Parsons screamed frantically as the creature tore flesh from bone. The screams stopped suddenly when the creature ripped his throat out, and then Harris saw the creature turn toward them.

The blood that still spurted from Parsons' neck drenched the animal's chest and face. It growled and pulled back its lips to reveal wickedly sharp teeth that seemed too large for its mouth. It had once been a large dog, but not anymore. Its paws had large talons protruding so far out that the creature rested on their points rather than the paw itself. Harris saw all this in an instant, and then the creature leapt again. Its speed was so great that it seemed to simply disappear.

Men started to scatter, but in the landing's close confines they merely tripped over each other. Two fell down the stairs. Harris tripped over the severed arm of one of his companions and fell backward into one of the bedrooms. He watched the creature land on top of two other men and then lost sight of it as he hit the floor. The smell of blood and faeces made him gag. He clawed his way back to his feet, only to slip again on the gore that covered the floor. The creature finished gorging on its latest victim and then, as if on cue, turned to face him.

Harris backed up frantically, brought his gun to bear and pulled the trigger. He screamed continually as the gun bucked in his hands, and his finger still gripped the trigger long after he had run out of bullets. The force of the shots threw the creature against the far wall, and blood and gore splattered the surface with sprays of colour. Harris grinned, his face maniacal with fear, blood and triumph.

The landing area was a charnel house; bodies and parts of bodies were everywhere. Harris couldn't even make out the number of dead in the pale light. Just then the creature stirred and, with a shake of its head, stood up. It was covered in blood, but its wounds had already closed. Its eyes were deep red and it glared at Harris.

"Jesus!" Harris gasped and backed away. His foot caught on one of the bodies and he tripped. This time he reached out to grab at anything for support. His hands touched material, the drape, and he grabbed it with all his might to avoid falling. The creature sprang into the air and crashed into Harris. Both of them fell to the ground. Harris maintained his grip on the drape as he fell. The material ripped along the rod and light suddenly filled the room. The creature recoiled and yelped with pain.

Harris was on his back, looking straight up at the thing. Its flesh contracted over the bone and wisps of smoke appeared all over its body. The creature swung its head from side to side frantically, its teeth passing inches from Harris' face. He was afraid that if he tried to shove the creature off, those teeth would rip him to pieces, so he remained still and watched as the thing howled and melted above him.

"Harris!" He heard the shout, but it sounded far off at first.

"Harris!" It was closer this time, but still faint. He felt hands claw at him, a veil seemed to lift from his eyes, and then he saw Henshaw.

"Christ you're a mess." Henshaw smiled down at him and wiped the ichor from Harris' face and clothes. The smell hit Harris then and he nearly passed out from the stench.

"What was that thing?" Harris asked.

"Fucking vicious is what it was," Henshaw quipped and helped Harris to stand up. The smile died on Harris' face when he saw the hallway.

"How many?" he asked.

"We've got four dead here and two outside," Henshaw dropped his head. "Kelly and Ashley are still on guard out front."

"Come on, we have to finish this."

The two men slowly ascended the stairs, their bodies tense, and ready to react to the slightest movement. On the third level hall they found more carnage.

I didn't even know their names, Harris thought as he made his way through the gore. "Be careful," he whispered, "there might be another one of those creatures."

Of the three rooms on the last floor, the first two turned up empty. The two men were petrified, their clothes were soaked with sweat and their hearts hammered in their chests. Harris pointed to the last door and both men prepared to enter. Henshaw put up three fingers and began to count down by closing each one in turn. On the last count both men kicked the door and barged into the room.

"At last," Henshaw whispered. The coffin was in the middle of the otherwise empty room. Both men relaxed and approached the casket. Henshaw pulled the drapes and let the sunlight flood the room. They nodded to each other and gripped the lid at each end. The two men covered in blood and dust smiled at each other in triumph despite the ordeal. They lifted the cover up, sent it crashing to the floor and looked down.

Empty.

"Bollocks!" Harris swore and then noticed a blinking LED screen at the far end of the coffin.

"Oh, Shit." Henshaw saw the box at the same time, then saw the display.

5 Seconds.

Harris knew they wouldn't make it down the stairs. He sprinted toward Henshaw, caught the other man in a low tackle, and continued on to crash through the window behind him. The two men flew through the air just before the room exploded. Dust and debris flew after them as they plummeted the three stories to the garden below.

CHAPTER
FIFTEEN

Warkowski made his way through the city. The streets were deserted, but he kept to the shadows as much as possible. The sounds of battle raged behind and each gunshot, each scream, tore at him. He didn't like leaving his position, letting his new friends down, but to be so close to Sarah and Jill and to do nothing was unbearable.

Jill was only nine years old, their pride and joy. Her long fair hair reached down to her waist, despite her many efforts to train it into curls. Warkowski could still see her pretty little face scrunched up, her lips beginning to tremble, as she removed the rollers in the morning only to have any curls fall out. Her hair remained stubbornly straight. She was the image of her mother, the same high cheekbones and deep blue eyes that Warkowski had fallen in love with ten years before when he had first met Sarah.

"I'm coming, Sarah," he whispered and continued resolutely to their old apartment.

Dawn was beginning to take hold on the city when Warkowski turned the corner into the street. He could see the window to their old apartment and his heart thundered in his chest.

Are they here? Are they alive? The thoughts raced around his head, consumed him, and he picked up the pace. His stomach tied itself in knots and he broke into a run. He was so intent on the building he didn't notice the patrol until he literally crashed into the first thrall.

The two men tumbled to the ground. Warkowski was totally unprepared for the impact and he felt the air rush from his body when he fell across the thrall. He lay on the ground and sucked air, trying to feed his starved lungs. The thrall recovered quickly and sprang back to his feet with a nimbleness that belied his rather portly physique.

"Look what we have here." The thrall directed his comment at someone out of Warkowski's field of vision. "We don't need that," he said indicating the machine gun, "let's have a bit of fun."

"But the alarm, we have to go," the second thrall complained.

"Don't worry; this'll only take a minute." With that he planted a kick into Warkowski's ribs that lifted him clear off the ground and sent him sprawling against an abandoned car. Warkowski felt a rib break and pain shot through his body. His vision blurred and then he felt himself being lifted by the thrall. "These humans are so frail," the thrall laughed.

Warkowski coughed up all the phlegm he could muster and spat into the thrall's face. The spit was laced with blood. He looked up at the window of his apartment. *So close,* he thought, and then he was flying across the street again. He landed on his face and scraped the skin against the road. Cuts opened all along his cheek and he felt himself loose consciousness.

The thrall laughed and approached him again. Warkowski pressed against the area around his broken rib to make the pain act as an anchor. His head cleared. He watched the thrall approach and steeled himself for one last effort. The second thrall followed the first tentatively, but stayed some ten feet behind.

"Peters, we really have to go. Hammond will feed our guts to the hounds if we don't report back." Warkowski listened to the second thrall complain and nearly laughed that the fearsome brute should have such an ordinary name.

"Relax. Look, he's begging now." The thrall laughed again and pointed at Warkowski as the man made his way to his knees. "Should I put him out of his misery?"

As the thrall came closer, Warkowski allowed himself to fall forward, pleading and using the thrall's clothes to scramble up. The thrall went to brush the pleading human away, but Warkowski slipped a grenade from his belt, pulled the pin and stuffed the explosive down the thrall's open shirtfront. The thrall looked quizzically at the human, and then blanched when Warkowski showed him the pin on his finger.

The thrall started a comic dance, stuffing his arms into his fatigues and trying desperately to get at the grenade. His companion looked totally confused, and in that moment of indecision Warkowski struck. He launched himself from the first thrall and ripped his knife from its scabbard. Even with its superior speed the thrall was taken by surprise when Warkowski rammed the knife through his neck and up into his brain.

The blood spurted everywhere after Warkowski pulled the knife from the wound and threw himself to the ground. He rolled as fast as he could away from the two thralls. The creature he had stabbed fell like a brick to the ground and lay unmoving. The second thrall still gyrated as he tried to locate the grenade. Warkowski rolled and rolled, the pain in his side secondary to his survival instinct. The explosion, when it came, was loud and very messy. Warkowski glanced back and saw the thrall's lower torso still standing in the middle of the road. The upper part, however, was splattered over the entire street.

"That's the problem with these bastards," Warkowski quipped, "one little rejection and they fall to pieces."

Warkowski felt as if each step he took toward the building stuck a knife into his side. The door was locked, of course. He spent a further few minutes kicking the door until it finally gave way and slammed against an internal wall. Glass shattered with the force and littered the floor of the foyer.

"Three floors," he muttered as he looked at the stairwell in despair, "why couldn't we have lived on the ground floor?" He gritted his teeth and began the long, painful climb. On the second floor landing he slumped against the wall and looked at his watch, shocked to see that he had taken seven minutes to climb this far. He was now about five minutes behind schedule and knew he'd be a lot later by the time he got the girls out in his condition. He pushed himself away from the wall and continued his climb.

When he finally reached the door to his apartment he hesitated. All his doubts, fears and dreams crashed into him with a physical force that made him stagger. The last few weeks of worry about his family had affected him badly. Would they be safe, or even alive, when he got there? His whole body ached, not just physically from the beating he had taken, but it was emotionally drained from the weeks of worry. He looked at the door knowing that all the answers lay on the other side. All he had to do was enter.

His hands shook when he reached for the handle.

Locked

"You dumb shit," he berated himself "of course it's locked." He took a deep breath, steeled himself, and rammed his shoulder into the door. Pain shot through his side and he stifled a scream. He put all his weight again and again against the door until the pain became a dull constant. Finally, the door flew open and he stumbled into the room.

There in front of him stood Sarah and little Jill. Relief flooded through him at the sight and he moved toward them.

"You're okay," he rejoiced and grinned.

Both of the girls cowered, though it was more of a flinch because the serum prevented them from responding fully. Warkowski stopped when he saw the fear in their eyes.

"Sarah, it's me," he stammered, confused that they would be afraid of him. "Don't you recognise me?"

Just then he caught his reflection in a mirror behind the two girls. His face was streaked in blood and dirt. The cuts on his cheek still bled and his body was covered in gore and blood.

Most of it's not mine, thank God, he thought. He looked hellish and couldn't blame Sarah for not recognising this gore-spattered figure that had violently entered their home.

"Sarah, it's me," he repeated. He raised his hands and slowly approached them.

Sarah's face didn't change, but her eyes suddenly grew wider. Warkowski could see recognition replace the fear, and then a softness that he thought he would never see again. A single tear fell from her left eye. Warkowski was amazed that she could portray such emotion with the serum blocking her bodies' reactions. His own tears welled up as he scooped both of them into his arms and hugged them tightly.

The pain was intense but he didn't care. He hugged them, kissing their foreheads as relief flooded through him. He left dark stains on their skin from the mix of dirt and blood, but they still looked beautiful. Tears flowed freely down his face. They couldn't hug him back. He knew that, but that would come later when they got that damn serum out of them. For now it was enough just to feel them in his arms. Later they would make their way back to the meeting point, but for now this was enough.

CHAPTER
SIXTEEN

"Drop your weapons." The words reverberated around the room.

John Pritchard was behind the door when he heard the command. He quickly ducked behind a filing cabinet and peeped out to see a rather stocky thrall issue the command with obvious relish and his weapon was leveled evenly at Scott Anderson. The five other thralls quickly spread out behind him and covered the rest of the small group. The thralls' arrival had caught them completely by surprise. He watched as Scott gave the signal to the others to comply and dropped his own machine gun with a sigh. Bill Anderson threw his weapon down in disgust. Jenny White, who wasn't actually armed, laid down the bags she carried anyway. Hackett merely placed his weapon at his feet with a resigned shrug.

"How can you work for those bastards?" Scott Anderson asked. Pritchard wasn't certain, but he thought that Scott had seen him duck behind cover. The fact that Scott was directing attention at himself and away from Pritchard was a good sign. He pressed himself further against the wall and listened to the exchange.

"Oh, it's not really so bad," the stocky thrall replied. "They leave us pretty much alone to do as we like, and I do mean whatever we like." He winked lasciviously and the others thralls grunted agreement.

"But you're human," Scott countered.

"Oh, not anymore we're not. We're so much more than that now. We're stronger and faster than ever before, and we're the ones in control."

Thoughts raced through Pritchard's mind. He explored every avenue he could think of to rescue something from the fiasco they found themselves in. Stupid, he chastised himself, we should have had a guard on the door.

As silently as he could he searched the bag he carried. He quickly disregarded the two grenades he found. They would probably do too much damage and injure his friends in the blast. Just then his hands found a slightly larger, misshapen grenade and he looked up to the ceiling and offered a prayer of thanks.

The thrall rambled on about being more than human and Pritchard risked a quick peek. He had to give Scott some warning if his new plan was to have any chance of working. He looked around the edge of the cabinet and immediately saw that all the thralls were gathered close together. Like fish in a barrel, he thought. He brought the flash grenade out just past the edge of the cabinet and caught the slow nod from Scott.

"Wait a minute."

Pritchard heard the shout interrupt the argument, but didn't recognise the voice

"There were five of them. Where's the other one?"

Shit! He thought. *It's now or never.*

The grenade fell to the ground and everyone turned automatically to the noise. Scott Anderson shut his eyes tightly just before the flash grenade exploded and had already hit the floor before the blinding light filled the room. He landed on his arm and grunted with pain. He opened his eyes. The intense light was gone, but the thralls still screamed in pain and crashed about with their hands to their eyes. He saw Pritchard came out from behind the cabinet. The sound of his machine gun was deafening in the small room. He looked about frantically for a weapon.

There, he thought. He saw the butt of his machine gun over to his left about five feet away and rolled over to the weapon. His shoulder hurt like hell, but he ignored the pain and scooped up the weapon. He checked the magazine and opened fire.

They never really had a chance. The crossfire of bullets caught the thralls in a deadly hail and they jerked violently with each impact. Bullets whined around the room, and Scott saw Hackett clutch his eyes and drop blindly to the floor. His brother, over by the window, blinked furiously and then launched himself at Jenny White, taking both of them to the relative safety of the floor.

The bald man who had shouted earlier wasn't so lucky. He screamed as two bullets ripped into him. The first impacted just below the jaw line and ricocheted off the bone to continue on through his brain. The soft flesh didn't even slow the bullet down and it exited out the back of his skull. The second round plowed into his left shoulder and sent the man spinning across the lab table. He was dead before his body fell to the ground.

Pritchard stopped firing as the last thrall fell.

"Let there be light," he sang in his best AC/DC impression

"What kept you?" Scott Anderson winked at him and picked himself up to survey the damage.

"Oh, and I thought you were getting on so well with these guys." Pritchard crossed the room and helped Jenny and Bill Anderson to their feet. They both blinked profusely and rubbed at their eyes, trying to get rid of the spots swirling in front of them. "Don't worry it'll pass," he assured them and bent down to retrieve their belongings.

Over by the wall he heard Scott help Hackett to his feet and only then noticed the other white-coated technician.

"What's your name?" he demanded.

"R...Roberts," the man stammered in reply.

"Well, Roberts, it's your lucky day. You've just joined the resistance."

Harris felt the air rush past him while he fell. Henshaw was still slumped over his shoulder from the tackle, still dazed from taking the brunt of the impact through the window, and Harris tried to turn in mid-air to avoid his friend taking the full impact. Amazingly he had time to think of Butch Cassidy and the Sundance Kid making their famous leap over the waterfall before the impact came and darkness enveloped him.

John Kelly jumped when the explosion came. He looked up in time to see two men crash through the third floor window and fall toward him. They seemed to twist in the air, and then they hit the ground with a sickening thud.

Neither moved.

"Oh, Jesus," Kelly muttered as he ran to the two figures. His hands quickly found the artery in Henshaw's neck and he sighed when he found a faint pulse. "This one's still alive," he shouted to Ashley as the man approached. "See if you can make him comfortable, but for God's sake don't move him."

Kelly had already moved on to the other figure. His hands searched for a pulse. "Oh no," he whispered when his fingers detected nothing. He clasped his fingers together and pumped Harris' chest, counted, then pressed again. He stopped to blow into Harris' mouth and then checked again for a pulse.

Nothing.

"Come on, Harris," he urged while he continued CPR. Push, count, blow and then a second time, push, count, blow. Sweat ran freely from his brow and he became more desperate. He straddled Harris and used all his weight to pump against his chest. "Come on, you bastard. You can't die on us now."

Harris suddenly jerked and made a loud rattling noise as he sucked air into his starved lungs.

"Thank God," Kelly sighed. "Don't try to move yet. We have to see what damage you've done." Kelly gently patted along Harris' body and watched for any reaction. Harris' left arm was bent behind him at an unnatural angle and Kelly lifted him gently to free the limb. Harris gritted his teeth as pain swept over him and he nearly passed out again.

"Okay," Kelly soothed, "it looks like you got off lightly. Your left arm is fucked, but the rest of you seem to be okay. Can you try sitting up?"

"I didn't know that 'fucked' was an official medical diagnosis." Harris winced when he tried to sit up.

"It is when you're dealing with crazy bastards who jump out of windows," Kelly replied. "How do you feel?"

"Dizzy," Harris replied.

"Okay, stay there and it'll pass." Kelly turned to Ashley. "How is Henshaw?" he asked.

"He's awake, but he says he can't lift his legs."

"Henshaw," Kelly bent over the prone figure, "I'm going to lift you to a sitting position, so hold on." Henshaw screamed when Kelly lifted his shoulders.

"Pain is a good sign," Kelly encouraged, "it means you're not paralysed."

Harris looked over to his friend and the two men grinned at each other.

"Anything that doesn't kill ya only makes you stronger," Henshaw managed between gritted teeth. "I really hate to bring this up, but how the hell are we going to get back to the meeting point in this state?"

Kelly scratched his head and looked around, and then a broad grin appeared on his face. "Wait there, I have an idea."

With that he sprinted across the street and disappeared behind the house. Harris lifted his left arm across his body and laid it in his lap to look at his watch.

Five minutes late already, he thought, *we'll never make it at this rate.*

CHAPTER
SEVENTEEN

T he burst of fire impacted the table that Reiss hid behind and sprayed debris into his eyes. He recoiled back behind the cover and looked around him to gauge how many of his men were still alive. Rodgers lay over by the stairs with his arm cradled in his lap. Tyson and Williams lay crumpled against the far wall; the angle of their necks left no doubt as to their condition. Fischer, Price and Wentworth all scrambled for whatever cover they could find. The others all lay still and Reiss couldn't tell whether they were alive or dead.

He briefly considered using a grenade, but in these close confines the blast would damage both parties. He rolled to his right, pointed his machine gun in the thralls' general direction and pulled the trigger. The thralls answered his fire and drove him back behind his cover.

Damn! He thought. *This isn't getting us anywhere.*

Suddenly a door opened at the top of the stairs and three thralls appeared. They opened fire and Price and Wentworth screamed as bullets ripped through them. Fischer made a break for the window to try to avoid the deadly crossfire but, unfortunately, got caught by both sides and bullets thumped into his body. The thralls neared the end of the stairs and Reiss knew that they'd see Rodgers any second. He shouted a warning and let loose a sustained blast. He ignored the bullets that ricocheted around him and smiled in satisfaction when he saw two of the thralls fall and tumble down the remaining steps.

The thralls behind Reiss used the distraction to their advantage and advanced on his position before he could bring his weapon around. Bullets flew all around him, destroying the furniture in front of him. The volume of fire became too much. "All right, all right, I surrender!" he shouted over the racket and threw his weapon down.

The remaining thrall from upstairs reached the ground floor and kicked Rodgers viciously. He even spat on the wounded man as an added insult. The lead thrall grabbed Reiss and threw him roughly to the ground. When he thought about it later he realised that act probably saved his life.

The back door suddenly flew open and he caught a brief glimpse of Jenkins before bullets again decimated the small foyer. The noise was thunderous as bullets strafed around the room. Bodies jerked violently in a grotesque dance and then fell to the ground. Reiss remained on the ground with his hands over his head until Jenkins approached him and signaled the all-clear.

Reiss got to his feet and looked around him at the new carnage.

My God, how many have to die before this nightmare ends, he thought. He went to help Rodgers.

"We've got two more alive here," Jenkins said as he examined some of the unmoving team members. "That makes twelve still alive, but only six mobile for now."

He saw some of the men picking themselves up around the room and staggering over to help team-mates.

Twelve still alive still means eight dead, Reiss thought. *Eight good men dead in*, he looked at his watch, *only twenty minutes.* "Okay, people," he said, "those who can walk, follow me. Rodgers, get the wounded to the trucks. We've still got to get those supplies out and we've just run out of time."

Warkowski led his family through the streets as quickly as his broken ribs would allow. The morning light had burned away all the shadows so they kept to the side streets as much as possible. He hoped they didn't meet a patrol. The girls could only walk at a slow pace and his own appearance would be impossible to hide. He cursed the serum for the umpteenth time that night.

He was already ten minutes late.

If all had gone to plan, his colleagues would have loaded up and left at this stage, but he had to believe that his sacrifices over the last hour counted for something, and he continued on, hoping that, somehow, they could still get home. In the distance he heard a strange scraping sound, metal on concrete, and he frowned. It wasn't any engine he had ever heard and, intrigued, he led the girls in the direction of the noise.

The noise grew louder. He motioned for the girls to stay put while he continued on to investigate. Just ahead of him, about a hundred and fifty yards down the street, he saw three men struggling to pull a car hood. The metal scrapped along the concrete in short spurts and their exertion was obvious even at this distance. A third man walked along beside them, helping at intervals, but was himself injured and of little help.

"That's Harris!" Warkowski muttered. The feeling of elation was quickly squashed by the realisation that he was here without permission. He could ignore the struggling party and go around. Even at his slow pace he would be at the meeting point before Harris, but he knew he could not do that. The men needed his help and, despite leaving his position earlier, Warkowski did not consider himself a quitter or a deserter. He rushed back to his family and led them out of hiding to hail the group ahead.

"Harris!" he shouted.

The three men stopped and looked to the source of the shout.

"Who is that?" Ashley asked. He squinted, trying to focus on the approaching figures.

"Isn't that Warkowski?" Kelly replied. "But who's that with him?"

Harris waited for the three figures to approach and looked at the two girls before he locked Warkowski in a withering gaze. "You couldn't wait."

Warkowski couldn't hold the gaze and dropped his eyes to his feet as he shifted uncomfortably. "I'm sorry, Harris. I really am, but I couldn't bear to think of them in this hellhole alone. To be so close and do nothing . . ."

His voice trailed off and Harris watched Warkowski put his arm protectively around his family. He was a bear of a man, his arms as thick as tree trunks, but Harris could see the tenderness with which he treated them.

"You better hope nobody dies because you left your post." Harris stared at Warkowski, his eyes hard as steel, and then his face softened. "How are they?"

"Petrified. That damned serum. Goddamn it, Harris, what kind of monster traps people in their own bodies like that? She's only nine years old," he replied. Tears of frustration welled up in Warkowski's eyes, and thin rivulets crept down his blood-encrusted face.

"You look as bad as I feel," Harris said softly. "Come on, put her on our carriage and let's get out of here. We're already way too late."

Warkowski scooped up his daughter in his arms as if she weighed nothing and laid her gently on the hood with Henshaw. He then moved around front and took up position. The sound of metal scraping on concrete began again and its echo reverberated through the empty streets.

Jenkins led the way down the stairs to the basement. The rest of his team followed, favouring different injuries.

What a sorry group we make, Reiss thought while he watched his team stumble and limp its way to the supplies. *I hope we don't meet any more thralls.*

The group spread out once they reached the bottom and approached the racks of food and supplies that filled the majority of the basement area.

"My God, I've never seen so much food in one place. We've hit the jackpot, guys." Jenkins grinned like a cat in a creamery.

"Okay, people, let's get to work," Reiss ordered. "Oh, Jenkins, when you drop off the first load at the trucks send the drivers back here to help. The wounded can mind the vehicles. We need every able bodied man to shift this lot."

They went to work.

They'd been moving the supplies for ten minutes when they heard the distant rumble.

"Did you hear that?" Jenkins asked.

"Yea, it never ends, does it?" Reiss replied and grabbed his machinegun. "You guys continue with this and I'll check it out."

He disappeared up the stairs, exited out to the street and ran towards the approaching noise. When he reached the end of the street he skidded to a halt. The noise was deafening this close. Reiss risked a quick glance around the corner, then blanched and collapsed back against the wall in shock.

"Jesus, a tank."

Harris lay in a gully and watched while the tank thundered down the narrow street. There wasn't much room for it to maneuver so it crushed any cars and debris in its path. Its progress was slow, thankfully, but it was advancing steadily and would be in range soon.

"Warkowski, get Henshaw and the girls out to the trucks and warn the others. Kelly, Ashley, follow me." The men hurried to their assigned tasks and Harris' heart hammered in his chest while he watched the approaching behemoth. It can't get much worse, he thought wryly.

It was at that point that he heard the helicopter.

Warkowski stumbled over the debris made by their initial assault and saw the trucks. Sweat poured from his body and his ribs ached from the exertion of carrying Henshaw and Jill, but still he smiled when he saw the men loading the supplies.

"We'll have you safely tucked up in bed soon," he whispered to his daughter and kissed her lightly on the forehead.

He made his way down to the vehicles and laid his charges in the furthest truck. The other two were completely full with supplies. He hugged his family with intensity and then turned to one of the men.

"Take care of them." He spoke softly and without apparent menace, but the soldier swallowed hard when he saw the look on Warkowski's face. Without waiting for a reply Warkowski turned and headed back up through the ruined wall.

When he reached the top he glanced back briefly and then snapped his head forward when he heard a thunderous blast that was followed closely by a high-pitched whine. Then the wall in front of him disappeared. The explosion picked him up and he felt himself fly through the air before being slammed hard against the remains of the wall.

After that he felt nothing.

Sarah Warkowski watched impassively as the explosion lifted her husband and tossed him like a rag doll against the wall. Her features remained unchanged, but inside she exploded. Years of serum-induced passiveness started to crumble as the pure, raw emotion welled up inside and overpowered the chemical's effect. A tidal wave of emotion gathered strength deep inside her and built to a crescendo. Just when she felt she would burst, the emotion was released in one long sustained scream.

"Noooooo!"

The scream trailed off as the exertion took its toll. Her eyes rolled behind her eyelids and Sarah Warkowski collapsed.

Reiss ran back to the police station in shock. "Okay, everyone," he shouted down the steps, "grab what you can carry, this is the last run."

"What's up?" Rodgers asked while he struggled one-handed with his burden.

"There's a tank outside," Reiss said breathlessly.

All activity stopped for a second as the full impact registered.

"You're shitting me," Rodgers exclaimed. Suddenly, there was a loud boom and the whole building shook when the west wall of the station collapsed. The violence of the attack galvanized the men into action.

"Get to the trucks as fast as you can. Hurry!" Reiss shouted and then turned and disappeared back out to the street.

The tank had made it to the top of the street. Reiss arrived at the door in time to see another shell explode over by the outer wall. He saw a figure thrown against the wall and lie unmoving against it.

"Poor bastard," he whispered. He reached out a hand and stopped Rodgers. "Ken, they'll never make it. We have to stop that tank."

Rodgers looked at Reiss and nodded. "Let's do it."

Scott Anderson and his party quickened their pace when they heard the first explosion.

"Jenny, you and Hackett take Roberts and the supplies out the way we came in. John, Bill, let's go see if we can do anything to help."

Hackett nodded and took the extra packs from the others, offloading some of these onto Roberts, who teetered violently with the extra weight. "Be careful," Hackett called after them and then led his charges off to the east.

The three men nodded and rushed off toward the sounds of battle.

The helicopter buzzed across the square, its twin heavy machine guns blazing and sending parallel streams of death into the retreating men. Some of the men stopped, dropped the supplies they carried and began firing back. Bullets filled the air and Reiss watched while more of his men died, their bodies torn apart by the high calibre bullets.

All the time the tank rumbled closer.

"Rodgers, I don't suppose you could make this easy and rustle up some more rounds for that Bazooka?" he asked, indicating the discarded weapon.

"'Fraid not, sir. That only happens in cheap novels."

The helicopter finished its run and pulled up high over the surrounding buildings in preparation for another run. Three more bodies lay still on the ground and the rest of the men scrambled over the rubble, desperate to get out of the killing ground.

"If he sees the trucks this will have all been for nothing."

"I know."

And with that the two men stepped out.

CHAPTER
EIGHTEEN

Harris stood in an alleyway behind the tank and watched the huge machine trundle past. A number of thralls trotted in its wake and made Harris press further back into the shadows.

"How many?" Ashley asked.

"About fifteen," Harris replied, "but you can be sure there's more to come. Are you up for this?"

Kelly and Ashley hefted the grenades in their hands and nodded.

"I keep thinking of Butch and Sundance," Harris muttered.

"What's that?"

"Nothing," he said. "Now or never then, guys." With that, the three men came out from behind the wall and all hell broke loose.

The men threw their grenades quickly and brought their weapons to bear even before the first blast ripped through the thralls. Bodies were flung into the air by the blasts, the explosions popping like firecrackers at second intervals, and then the machine guns roared and caught the thralls in a devastating crossfire.

The thralls were taken by surprise, but their reactions were uncanny. Boosted by their enhanced abilities, a few managed to get their guns ready and return fire at the three men. Bullets flew past Harris' head and his shirt billowed as the rounds tore at the material. Beside him he heard Ashley scream when a line of bullets stitched a pattern from his groin to his neck. Harris suddenly fell to one knee when his left leg was shot from under him and then, just as suddenly as it began, it was all over.

The tank continued on its way, oblivious to the brief and deadly battle behind. The air was full of the smell of blood and cordite and Harris gagged on each breath.

"Are you okay?" Kelly asked.

Harris looked over at Ashley.

"He's dead, I'm afraid," Kelly confirmed.

Harris just nodded and began to climb to his feet using the machine gun for support. "Come on, we're not done yet."

Reiss and Rodgers stood side by side in the street and watched the helicopter bank in readiness for its return run. Behind them the rest of their group had reached the top of the rubble and disappeared down to the trucks. Both men checked their magazines and slapped the chambers closed. The helicopter straightened its approach and opened fire. Bullets traced a line some fifty yards ahead of the two men, picking up small tufts of dirt and asphalt with each impact.

Scott Anderson could see the two men in the middle of the street. The scene was one of nightmares and war movies. Fires burned steadily all over the square. The whole area appeared to be under a shadowy veil of thick smoke mingled with the dust from the destroyed buildings that blocked the morning's sun. The noise of the tank and the helicopter were deafening and he shuddered at the sheer horror of the scene.

"What the fuck are they doing?" Pritchard asked from behind.

"Trying to distract the helicopter so the trucks can get away," Anderson shouted back.

Pritchard blanched.

"Right, you two set up here and fire at that fucker as soon as he's in range," Scott ordered and got to his feet. "Don't stop till he's either dead or you run out of bullets."

The helicopter had already begun its run and bullets tore up the road.

"What are you going to do?" his brother shouted over the thunderous noise.

"Join them, what else?"

Harris and Kelly ran after the tank.

"Keep me covered!" Harris shouted. He gritted his teeth against the pain in his leg and launched himself at the back of the tank. He caught hold of the rear service ladder and quickly pulled himself aboard. The diesel fumes that assaulted him as he pulled himself over the filter grids made him retch and cough violently. Then, suddenly, he was clear. He took a few seconds to rest and breathe fresh air before he again pulled himself to his feet and continued on.

Harris skirted the main hatch as he inched his way along the vehicle. The tank pitched and rolled like a boat at sea. As it traveled over the many bumps and debris Harris found the going slow. His arm, though not broken from the fall, hurt like hell and he couldn't grip the handrail properly. He shuffled past the hatch and finally managed to get to the turret extension. Gingerly he lowered himself from the side panel to a horizontal position and straddled the turret.

This was the time he was most vulnerable. The occupants of the tank noticed him for the first time and reacted. Harris heard the bolt in the hatch behind him slide open; metal creaked when the port was swung open. Harris heard a roar of gunfire and couldn't help but flinch while he waited for the impact.

The bullets, however, were not aimed at him. Kelly shadowed the tank and watched Harris make his way to the front. He had seen the main port swing open and let loose a hail of fire at the thrall who appeared. Bullets ricocheted around the hatch. The thrall blanched and tumbled back into the main cabinet. A few seconds later, a hand appeared and shut the hatch.

Harris lay over the turret on his stomach with hands wrapped around the metal on either side and began to pull himself along. The occupants tried to shake their passenger off by driving over rubble and potholes. The tank pitched violently and Harris slipped. He frantically swiped at the turret to stop himself falling. He grasped the turret with his left arm and screamed with pain when the injured muscles protested. Sweat poured down his face; his feet bounced against the asphalt mere inches from the treads of the tank. His hand began to slip and he tried once more to lever his legs back over the turret.

He brought his right hand up and used its strength to lever his legs up. He gained a foothold with his right leg, but the bullet in his left thigh had left that leg practically numb. He moved his hips and upper arms and finally dragged the injured limb over the turret. He lay there hanging upside down from the turret and waited for the pain to subside. It was then that he felt the rumble in the turret and the metal suddenly spiked in temperature. The roar of the explosion competed for volume with the scream that ripped from his throat as searing heat shot through the length of the turret. It was a close call as to which was louder.

Reiss watched the line of bullets approach and brought his own weapon up. He aimed the machine gun along its sight and began to fire. The recoil hammered his shoulder in a rapid, rhythmic beat. Reiss tried vainly to keep the weapon steady while it bucked in his hands. He was dimly aware of the bullet trail getting closer. Then bullets whined past him and, suddenly, a violent impact knocked the air from him. He felt himself fall and struggled for breath. Then darkness descended.

Scott Anderson ran toward the men who had raised their weapons and begun firing as bullets stitched across the asphalt toward them. He heard the gunfire behind him when his brother and Pritchard joined the fray. There was no time to join the two men and they obviously were not aware that help had arrived. They had bet everything on this gambit. Scott ran harder and launched himself at the men. He caught Reiss in the midriff and his momentum carried them into Rodgers. The three men tumbled in a heap as the road where they had stood only moments before was ripped to shreds.

Bullets ricocheted off the metal of the helicopter. Pritchard shouted in triumph when a spider-web shattered across the glass screen in front of the pilot. Some of the bullets penetrated the glass and ricocheted madly within the small cabinet of the flight area. The helicopter seemed to shudder in the air and then the high-pitched drone of the engine missed a few beats. It coughed and spluttered until the engine died.

The blades continued to turn, but the engine driving them had given up by the time the machine dropped like a stone.

Harris felt the heat sear his hands and thighs, but knew he'd be crushed if he let go, so he held grimly on. The pain was intense, but luckily the metal cooled quite quickly once the shell passed. Harris renewed his effort to pull himself along the length of the turret. Blisters formed on his hands and legs and just as quickly burst. He had passed the point where the pain made any difference; now it just remained at a constant level.

The tank suddenly veered to the left and drove directly at a nearby building. Harris groaned when he realised that the thralls were trying a different approach. He saw the wall some twenty feet away and redoubled his efforts to get to the end.

Fifteen feet.

Harris pulled himself forward and smiled grimly when his ruined fingers touched the end of the turret.

Ten feet.

He reached back and pulled a grenade from his belt. His heart skipped a beat when the grenade nearly slipped in his blood-soaked hands. He gripped it tighter and ignored the pain from the blisters. The wall loomed closer as he brought the grenade to his mouth, gripped the pin with his teeth and pulled.

Five feet.

The wall was right in front of him when Harris stuffed the grenade into the bore of the turret and tried to launch himself to the ground. His body just didn't have the energy needed to get clear and the tank treads loomed above him. The turret hit the wall and exploded at the same time. Debris flew everywhere. Harris felt a strong grip under his left arm and suddenly he was pulled out from under the tank. The treads missed him by inches on their way past. Bricks and the remains of wooden supports rained down on him and his body took another beating. The turret itself split like a banana at the top from the explosion.

The tank, however, was still a dangerous tool. It changed gear and began to reverse out of the building.

Harris looked up and saw Kelly, who continued to pull him clear of the rubble. "Get the treads!" he shouted and waved the man away.

Kelly ran to the tank and pulled a grenade from his belt. The tank had freed itself from the wall and was already beginning to pull forward when Kelly pulled the pin and jammed it between the wheels. He returned to Harris and helped drag him to cover before the grenade exploded and tore the tread off the right wheel brace. The engine screamed and the smell of diesel hung heavy in the air as the thralls tried again and again to move the metal behemoth, but without the tread, the tank was just junk.

"Piece of cake," Harris quipped and then collapsed in Kelly's arms.

Pritchard and Bill Anderson ran over to the three men on the ground. Bill helped his brother get to his feet, while Pritchard checked on the other two.

"Anyone get the number of that truck?" Rodgers joked.

"Are you okay?" Pritchard asked. He helped Rodgers to a sitting position.

"I'll live," he replied. "How's Reiss?"

Pritchard looked over at Reiss and saw blood pour from a head wound. "Not so good," he replied. "Looks like one of those rounds grazed his head." He examined the wound and tore a strip from his shirt to tie it around Reiss' forehead. "We'll have to carry him. Are you up for it?"

"Okay, guys, quit the chatting," Scott Anderson interrupted. "Grab a leg and let's get out of here before the rest of the city shows up. Bill, check on the others and see if any are still alive."

The three men lifted Reiss and headed for the meeting point. Bill Anderson followed, stopping occasionally to check on the many still forms that littered the square. One after another Bill Anderson checked the bodies. His posture stooped further and tears welled in his eyes as, one after another, he found no sign of life. He reached the top of the mound of rubble made by their initial assault and turned back to look at the desolation.

So many dead, he thought. He turned to watch the others pull themselves into the last remaining truck. The failure to find anybody alive weighed heavily on him as he turned to join the others. Then, suddenly, he caught a movement out of the corner of his eye. He rushed over to the area where he saw the hand sticking up from the rubble. New hope replaced frustration as Bill fell to his knees and tore at the debris around the limb.

"Bill, come on. We're leaving." He heard the shouts from below, but ignored them. His hands bled and his nails cracked but, slowly, he revealed the body buried beneath.

"Warkowski," he exclaimed when he revealed the battered face. He pressed his fingers against the man's neck. "He's still alive." The pulse was weak but stable.

His heart leapt and he attacked the debris with renewed vigour, quickly clearing away the last of the rubble. He didn't have time to check the extent of the injuries, so he dragged the limp form and stumbled to the truck under its weight.

"Hold on, Warkowski. Don't you dare die on me."

CHAPTER
NINETEEN

H arris woke to pain. His whole body throbbed from the abuse of the last few hours. He opened his eyes and shut them again against the glare of the fluorescent lights. He tried again. This time he opened his eyes a mere crack and let them get used to the brightness. He was in the infirmary. The white plastic dividing curtains halfway round his bed and the metal bedpan on his locker were a dead giveaway. He turned his head to take in the whole room and pain once again swept over him.

"So you're awake?" He'd recognise that voice anywhere. Sandra. Harris gently turned to the sound of her voice and smiled when she came into view. Her face was creased with concern and black rings were visible beneath her eyes.

"Hi, gorgeous," Harris croaked, and Sandra Harrington smiled.

"You've been out for a while and the drugs we've pumped you with have dried up your throat. Don't worry, you'll be bawling out the troops again in no time."

"How long?" he asked. He made a face when his tongue stuck to the roof of his mouth.

"Twenty-four hours. Don't worry," she added quickly when she saw the alarm in his face, "we got all the supplies in without being seen. Pritchard and Kelly dumped the trucks miles away and returned a few hours ago. Looks like a job well done."

Sandra's smile faltered when she saw the pain on Harris's face. This pain she knew had nothing to do with the trauma his body had gone through.

"You couldn't have done any more, Peter."

"How many?" he asked.

"Seventeen didn't come back and three more are in here with you."

"Oh Jesus," he gasped and brought his right hand to his face.

"How's Warkowski?"

Sandra dropped her head, unable to give the news while looking at him. "He's alive." She tried to continue, but Harris put a hand on hers and stopped her. She looked up into his eyes, their sunken appearance gave him a haunted look, but he smiled encouragement. "We're doing everything we can," she said. "Sarah, that's his wife, hasn't left his bedside since they brought him in. She still can't talk with the serum's effects but she refuses to move."

Harris nodded. "How are the kids?" Sandra immediately brightened and Harris was relieved to see that familiar spark return.

"Oh, Peter," she enthused, "they're bouncing back already. We're having trouble keeping them in bed." Her smile was infectious and Harris felt the edges of his own mouth twitch. He lifted the covers and began to roll his legs over the side of the bed, but paused when his head swam.

"Where do you think you're going?" Her smile faded in a second and was replaced with such a stern look that Harris balked. "You will stay there until you've healed if I have to tie you to the bed," she ordered.

"Promises, promises," Harris smiled wistfully. "If I'd known you were into that I could have picked up a pair of handcuffs in town." Her hand made a swipe for him and he moved to avoid the playful slap. The muscles in his neck shrieked in protest and he grimaced.

"Oh, I'm sorry, I…"

"It's all right," he assured her and lay back in the bed. "My fault."

"That's better," she allowed. "Now I'm going to check on the kids. Stay put."

Harris watched her disappear through the doors. As soon as she had gone he pulled back the covers and rolled off the bed. He grabbed the plastic curtain to steady himself, and then, slowly, he hobbled out of the infirmary.

Harris stopped briefly at his room to change, a task that proved difficult with his hands so heavily bandaged. His shirt was unbuttoned and stuffed untidily into his pyjama bottoms. He had to stop frequently to lean against the wall, but he slowly made his way to the lab. He knew that he should be back in bed, but he had to know what had happened since the raid.

Seventeen dead. The number swirled around his head. They had been his responsibility and he needed something, anything, positive to have come out of the raid. At least then he might be able to convince himself that it had been worth it. The empty corridor confused him; normally the facility was a hive of activity.

Where is everyone? he wondered on his way to his destination. He thought that he might be dreaming at first, but the pain that racked his body with each step assured him that he was very much awake. He turned the corner to corridor "B" and saw the door to the lab. At the end of the corridor he noticed a digital display, red letters glaring against the stark, white background.

"3:15," he read. "No wonder it's so empty. They're all curled up in bed."

He wondered if he had wasted the journey and groaned inwardly when he thought about the long walk back, not to mention the disapproving look and lecture he was sure to get from Sandra. When he reached the lab door he noticed a faint light from within and turned the handle. When the door opened, he smiled with relief and stepped inside.

The interior was brightly lit. The whiteness of the tabletops and walls exaggerated the fluorescent lights and gave them an intensity that pained his eyes. Harris looked around and finally spotted his quarry amidst a jumble of paperwork and test tubes. The figure wrote furiously on a notepad and alternatively checked the eyepiece of a microscope.

"You look as happy as the proverbial pig in shit." Harris grinned and then regretted his outburst when the small man startled in shock and nearly overbalanced and fell off his chair.

"Peter, my dear boy." Pat Smith beamed when he recognised Harris. "I didn't know they'd let you out."

"Let's keep that one between us for now." Harris smirked.

"Oh, I see." Smith winked conspiratorially. "Well, it's good to see you whatever the circumstance."

Harris and Smith had become great friends in the last few weeks. What had started as a common interest, the defeat of the creatures through some chemical miracle, had quickly blossomed into a mutual respect and friendship. They worked closely together and Harris was constantly reminded of his father by many of the things Smith said and did. Although they did not look alike, Harris could see the same vitality and exuberance in this little man that he remembered in his father before he had had his stroke.

"You don't get out much, then?"

"What?" Smith replied, confused, and then noticed the unmade bunk in the corner. "Oh, yes, well, you know once I get into something I just loose track of time. But enough of that. How are you?"

Harris could see the concern in the man's face and for the first time also saw the strain and tiredness there. He suddenly felt guilty that he had spent the last twenty-four hours asleep while Smith was here hunched over a microscope.

"Except for the need for a body transplant. How's the research on the vampire's blood coming?"

"Oh, that, yes, the coagulation factor of the plasma…"

"Pat, Pat," Harris interrupted with his hands raised, "in English please."

"What? Oh, right, well…" Harris smiled at the concentration evident on his friend's face. "Well, you remember before you left that we were looking at the relationship between the oil in wood and the breakdown of the vampires' metabolism?"

Harris nodded.

"I think I've identified the necessary components." Smith beamed when he dropped his bombshell.

"Are you serious?" Harris asked incredulously. "That's fantastic."

"Well, as far as I can tell," Smith continued, "I isolated all the elements of wood secretions and tried each one on the sample you brought back, and then combinations of a few of them. Now, apparently, the vampire blood breaks down quite quickly once it stops pumping around their bodies. Many of the cells had already begun to die while I was testing."

"Go on," Harris prompted more dubiously.

"I finally got a combination that completely broke down the parasitic cells and held them in stasis…"

"But that's wonderful," Harris interrupted.

"…or the cells may have broken down themselves due to natural deterioration. I can't be totally sure."

Harris' jaw dropped. "So where do we go from here?" he asked.

"Well unless we get another, fresher, blood sample, then all I can suggest is we test the oil component I developed."

"How are we going to do that?" Harris looked puzzled.

"Oh, didn't I tell you? I made up a batch of the oil and got some of the older children to help coat some ammunition with it."

"What…where…how many?" the questions tumbled over each other and Harris tried to sort all the facts into some logical order.

"Calm down, they're over there in the corner. Actually, I think the kids did rather well."

Harris tuned out his friend and hobbled across the room to look at the cache of ammunition in the corner. Machine gun magazines of various types and single handgun rounds littered the area.

There must be hundreds of rounds here, he thought. "But this is great," he enthused to his friend. "Well done."

"I can't guarantee it will work, you understand, but the theory is sound. I can't really do anything more on this project, so I've been testing the serum for…"

"The serum?" Harris interrupted. He grimaced when he whirled around too quickly.

"Didn't you know?" Smith replied. "That young fellow, what's his name? Blonde fellow…"

"Anderson."

"Anderson, yes that's the one. Well, he brought in a whole jar full."

"Oh my God. What have you found?"

"It's still too early to tell in detail, but it seems to be a curious mix of depressants, not unlike those used in violent mental cases, only at a higher dosage. The long-term effects of administering such doses are worrisome. Once I break down the elements I'll look into how to negate the effects at a quicker pace, but I also want to run tests on our people here to see if we can expect any surprises from…"

"There you are! I should have known." The words ricocheted around the room and the volume made Harris cringe.

"Oh, hi, Sandra," Harris said meekly.

"Don't you 'Oh, hi, Sandra' me, Peter Harris," she fumed. "What are you doing out of the infirmary?"

"Pat and I were just…"

Harris's voice trailed off as he indicated where his friend had been standing, but the man was gone. He looked around and saw the familiar figure busily working at his desk, apparently oblivious to what was happening around him.

"Traitor." Harris turned as gave Sandra a full, beaming smile. "I was just going."

He suddenly felt very tired from his exertions and hobbled slowly toward the door. Sandra Harrington's rigid pose softened somewhat as she saw how pale he had become and moved to help him. She took his arm and allowed him to lean against her.

"What am I going to do with you?" she sighed.

Sarah Warkowski sat by her husband's bedside in silence. In contrast to her outer calm, her mind raced with all that had happened in the last twenty-four hours. It was like she had been thrust into a raging hurricane in a small dinghy.

She felt completely out of her depth.

Her existence for the last two years had been ordered; hell, but ordered. Fully aware of her predicament, but completely incapable of any but the most basic movements, she had become almost comfortable in her routine. She shuddered and felt sick when she thought of her weekly visits to donate blood, to receive her serum, the constant harassment from the thralls and, worst of all, their frequent nightly visits.

She pushed those thoughts away and looked down at her husband. When he had burst into their apartment she hadn't recognised him. He looked more demon than human with blood spattered everywhere and she feared that Jill and herself would be killed. The worst part of the effect of the drugs was not being able to help or protect her daughter and, at the moment when Philip crashed through the door, every fibre in her body strained against the drugs to protect her.

The relief she had felt when she had finally recognised the blood-soaked figure was like a physical blow. He had come back to them, against all odds he had come back. She had felt the tears roll down her cheeks as he had gathered them up in his massive arms.

She looked down at her husband's sleeping form and the tears rolled down her face again. She still couldn't move to wipe them away, but she could make it difficult for others to move her by planting her feet firmly on the ground. She could feel the difference already and knew it wouldn't be long before she could take her husband and daughter in her arms and hug them for the first time in two years.

They had told her that Philip might not survive, that his body had been very badly damaged by the blast. But as long as he breathed there was hope. The signal that ran across the monitor screen beeped every time it spiked and testified that he was still alive. The sound reverberated around the empty ward while she sat.

And waited.

And hoped.

"How's that?" Sandra Harrington asked when she poked the man's side.

"Feels a bit better," Jack Walton replied.

"That's strange; I could have sworn that those ribs were broken yesterday when you came in. We don't have x-rays, but the discoloration and bruising were consistent with that. You were with Reiss' team weren't you?"

"Yes."

"How was it? What are vampires like up close?"

"Petrifying."

Sandra shrugged at the lack of response from her patient. Oh well, he's probably still shaken from the assault, she thought. He had come in with Reiss' team, covered in blood and with bad bruising to his side. The blood must have been someone else's because Sandra could not find any wounds on his body. The bruising on his side, however, had been very bad and she had bandaged him up to support his ribs. This morning, though, the bruising was nearly gone and his side wasn't that sore to touch. She shook her head in amazement.

"Well if that bruising is gone by tomorrow we'll let you out," she said and straightened his bed covers. She gave him a quick smile and moved off to check on her next patient.

"Nurse."

She turned. "Yes?"

"Could you turn down the lights in here?"

"Of course, any particular reason?" she queried.

"I'm sensitive to light."

CHAPTER
TWENTY

"These are trying times."

The words, though not particularly loud, filled the auditorium and demanded the attention of all present. Father Matthew Reilly stood on a raised platform at the head of an audience that included every member of the community, except for the few who still remained in the infirmary. Sandra Harrington looked around the gathering with concern. The mood was sombre, almost maudlin.

She thought back to the initial joy of the team's return and how it had quickly disappeared when the full cost of the assault had become obvious. Members of the community had rushed out to welcome the teams, herself among them, when the trucks had pulled up outside the facility. Everyone smiled and joked at their safe return. Without exception the welcoming committee stopped in shock at the team's bloodied and dirt-encrusted appearance. Men and women limped and hobbled from the trucks, and many had to be carried or supported by others. Silence reigned and the welcoming committee just stared, unsure what to do.

She had heard her father curse as he pushed his way through the crowd. "For God's sake don't just stand there, help them!" he thundered. He lifted one of the survivors into his arms and strode back through the crowd.

The spell seemed to break then and people rushed forward to help. Vince Crockett organised some teams to help the injured and others to unload the supplies. His fierce countenance and authoritative bearing ensured absolute obedience.

The hours that followed were a blur of activity. She worked relentlessly with her team to check all the injured. They did not have a doctor, but cuts were cleaned, broken limbs set and more serious injuries were handled to the best of their caring, but limited, abilities.

For the first hour she had constantly looked to the door of the infirmary, searching the faces of the injured and hoping to see Harris. She moved from patient to patient, working efficiently, and held back her emotions while each patient related their particular account of the hell they had been through. The sheer scale and horror of their stories shocked her. Her own fears that Harris might be dead threatened to overwhelm her. In fact, it wasn't until she saw Scott Anderson push his way through the crowds with the limp and battered body of Harris in his arms that she felt the tears run down her face.

There had been so much blood she hadn't known where to start. She gestured to Scott Anderson to place him on a nearby bed and immediately checked for a pulse. She remembered the feeling of relief when she had felt a weak but steady rhythm. She glanced over his body and gently checked for broken bones. She paid particular attention to his face and the colour of his lips. Internal bleeding had been her greatest fear, but the tint of his features was a good indicator that a sufficient level of blood flowed in his body. Satisfied that he was stable, she dried her tears with the back of her hand and set about cleaning away the blood and grime.

Over the last few days Sandra had noticed the community's deep shock in the aftermath of the assault, so much so that she had brought it up at the last committee meeting. She was seriously worried that the low moral would succeed where the vampires had failed and tear the community apart. To this end she had requested, and been granted, a public forum to try to allay fears, bolster moral and, more importantly, allow people to say goodbye. She hoped that this would rekindle the sense of community they had lost and give people the strength to move on from this tragedy.

"Times of exceptional hardship and suffering." She shook herself from her reverie and listened to Father Reilly continue. "But also of exceptional deeds and sacrifice. We gather here today in honour of all the men and women who took part in the assault, but especially for the seventeen whom we now mourn."

Father Reilly paused and Sandra could see him look out over the audience.

"They died, yes, but let us not forget why they died. They died so our children could live, so our families could eat and so we could survive. They also died free."

He spoke the last words loudly, and Sandra jumped when Reilly slapped his open hand on the podium to emphasise the point.

"It is right that we grieve. We have all lost family members or friends, but we must become stronger in our resolve, in our faith, if we are to take any comfort or meaning from their sacrifice. Do not dishonour their memory or their achievement. Do not give up. I ask you all now to join me in a prayer and the sacrament of the mass. Our Father who art in…"

The words of the prayer were familiar to everyone, and Sandra heard a low murmuring as some people tentatively joined in. Although not a practising Catholic herself, the words to the prayer were so deeply rooted in her that they sparked memories of happier times. The ritual of the mass gave her comfort and she could see people around her turn to those beside them, shake hands and hug.

Her eyes welled up in the emotion of the prayer. The atmosphere shifted. The feeling of belonging and community spirit they had enjoyed before began to return, and the volume of the recitation increased as everyone joined in the prayer. By the end of the mass tears rolled down every face she could see and the volume of the final response was deafening. Together, as a community, they finished the mass with one simple word. A word which had been used for centuries, a word of power, a word which embodied their right to survive, to mourn their dead and to continue on with an unshakeable resolve.

"Amen!"

"Okay, people. Let's settle down and get to it," Dan Harrington boomed. All eyes looked to him. Conversations finished and people coughed and straightened chairs while they settled down for the meeting. This committee meeting had been called as soon after the mass as was feasible. It had taken a further two days to ensure the full committee could attend, but the community was already beginning to come to terms with the tragedy.

"First of all, I'd like to thank Father Reilly for his service." People grunted and nodded heads in agreement. "His words struck a cord in all of us and the mood in the facility has improved immeasurably. Peter," he continued and nodded to Harris, "I appreciate you being here also, considering your condition."

Harrington looked over at the young man and grimaced.

My God, the older man thought, *he looks dreadful.*

Harris' face was deathly pale; in fact, the only colour visible at all in his pasty visage was from the cuts and bruises that dotted his features. Bandages covered his body; some of them stained red from the wounds beneath that still continued to seep.

Harrington hadn't realised he was that bad.

Sandra had argued bitterly against his attending, but Harrington had pressed hard because he needed the input of all the members. They had argued and she had called him a bully. She still glared at him from her position beside her patient. Harrington suddenly regretted his insistence.

He had always had a brusque manner. The qualities that made him a successful entrepreneur in his previous life were the very ones that had torn his family apart and driven his wife away. She had finally had enough of the business trips, broken promises and constant mood swings. He realised too late that, while he was magnanimous when deals went well, he had been argumentative and bloody-minded when things didn't go his way.

He had lived for his work and didn't notice how this affected his family until, finally, Pamela had packed, taken their daughter and left over ten years ago. He sighed regretfully as he remembered how he had thrown himself further into his work instead of rushing after them. He had built a huge empire and only realised how lonely he was when he sat at the top with no one to share it with.

He had contacted Pamela out of the blue two years ago and had been surprised that she had been happy to hear from him. Over the previous few years the only contact had been through solicitors. He had always been too busy. Slowly, he had begun the process of bridge building and then the war had begun. At first it was something that seemed far away and wouldn't affect them directly, so he had requested some time with their daughter to get to know her again. Pamela had been happy to comply and suddenly this twenty-five year old stranger appeared on his doorstep. The war quickly spiralled out of control and travel became impossible, so Sandra had stayed with him a little longer than planned.

He looked over at his daughter. They had initially stayed in touch with Pamela by phone but, as the war worsened, utilities were disrupted and they had lost contact. He had no idea if she was alive or dead now. He and Sandra had become close in the last few months, but sparks still flew and each of them still had much to learn about the other. He shook himself from the past and looked around the table before he continued.

"However, I needed you all here because, quite frankly, I don't know where we can go from here."

A low murmur rippled around the table and people looked at each other quizzically.

"Don't get me wrong—the haul we got from the raid was fantastic. But the cost was too high and that was with the element of surprise. Any further assaults will be expected. The food we have now will last us six months with rationing, but what do we do then?"

He paused to let his words sink in. His glance roamed around the table, pausing briefly at each committee member.

"We must increase the size of this community, and that means more and more forays into vampire territory. Up till now the thralls have been complacent and unwilling to mobilise on any large scale because, let's face it, we really didn't rate the effort. That will have changed after our last raid. We made fools of them and the vampires will probably cull the whole top level of their command structure in retaliation. That will also make the new commanders very fucking anxious to please. We've already seen an increase in patrols and I feel that this level of activity will remain for the long term."

"Peter," he said and turned his attention to Harris. "It's good to see you up and around, legally, that is." There was a gentle ripple of laughter and Harris shifted uncomfortably in his wheelchair. The chair had been Sandra's idea and had been non-negotiable. Most of the facility had heard of his walkabout from the infirmary and subsequent capture. "Maybe you could fill us in on your end of things."

"As you know," Harris began, "we had three objectives for the assault. Food and medicine were completed successfully, but Nero anticipated us. We had hoped to confuse things for a while by removing their command figure, but he's cleverer than that. I can't help thinking we tried to do too much and that I..."

"You can stop right there," Harrington interrupted. Sandra had come to him before their argument, worried at Harris' mood. She felt that he placed far too much blame on himself for the recent deaths and had asked her father to talk to him. Harrington could see from the anguish on Harris' face that she had been right to worry. He felt bad that he had not said something sooner.

"You can't put any of what happened on your own shoulders. In fact, from what I've heard, you did more than anyone could expect of one person. There aren't many men I know who would attack a goddamn tank single-handed."

He heard Sandra gasp and cursed himself when he realised that Harris had obviously edited that part from the story when he had told her of the assault. She looked at him with a look that would melt iron. Harrington knew that Harris would be in big trouble when she got him back to the infirmary.

"We decided on the plan as a group," Harrington continued in an attempt to cover his mistake, "and right or wrong, we pick up the pieces as a group."

Harris merely nodded and continued to stare at the floor.

"Son," he continued in a softer tone, "this is a war and, no matter how much we try to prevent it, people will die. You can't take responsibility for everyone."

Harrington saw Harris raise his head and look deep into his eyes before he nodded, more emphatically this time.

"We did get a few bonuses from the assault," Harris continued with renewed vigour. "Scott Anderson brought back a full jar of the serum. He also brought back a volunteer to help us understand how it works." Harris grinned as he said this. People smiled along with him, relieved to see the mood lighten.

"We also picked up a few stragglers who will be weaned off the serum's effects over the next few days. These were mostly women we found in the thralls' quarters." A scowl darkened Harris's face as he remembered the scene. "I think we got twelve in total, no, fourteen if you include Phil's family."

"How is Warkowski?"

"Not good, but he's still breathing. We haven't sent out any patrols since we got back, but I plan to send three two-man teams out tomorrow to see the lay of the land. That's about it for now."

"Thank you, Peter." Harrington looked next at Pat Smith. "Pat, I believe you've been busy. Perhaps you can fill us in."

"Yes, as I explained to Peter the other day, I have come up with a compound that could be effective against the vampires." His enthusiastic beam was so contagious that many people found themselves grinning along with him.

"Could be?" Vince Crockett's question, his scowl, and deep baritone voice acted like a splash of cold water.

"Yes, well, what I mean is that by the time I developed this particular batch, the vampires' blood we used had already begun to decompose. I can't be absolutely certain that the compound was the only factor which destroyed the cells." Smith was totally unprepared for this sort of questioning. He believed that the lab results alone were reason for celebration and he fumbled his way through the rest of the presentation. "But the theory is sound and the signs are good," he finished and looked nervously around the table.

"I hope you don't expect us to send out our men on that basis, Mr. Smith," Crockett scowled. "Or maybe you are prepared to go out with them."

"Settle down, Vince," Harrington interrupted. "Pat can't help it if the blood decomposed before he could finish testing, although you do have a point. We'll have to shelve the testing of the ammunition until we can do it in a controlled environment."

"What!" he saw Harris nearly launch himself out of his wheelchair, but a combination of pain and Sandra's firm hand held him in place.

"This could be the very weapon we need to turn the tide on this nightmare. You were right before, those bastards are lethal, their speed and strength are frightening, and anything that kills them at a distance is a Godsend."

"That's the problem, Peter," he continued, "it could be the weapon we need, but we just don't know for certain. We can't send men out on the off chance that it will work. For now we need to concentrate on other things."

Harris slumped back in his chair. The toll of the exertion had hit him hard. "Let's at least equip the patrols with the ammunition," Harris suggested, his voice barely audible. "That way if they encounter trouble it may help. It certainly can't harm them."

Harrington glanced at Crockett and received a nod. "Okay, that's reasonable. Pat, will you ensure that Vince receives a supply of the ammunition for the patrols?"

"Yes, of course," Smith replied, indignant that the question had to be asked at all.

"Good, that's settled. Any other business, Pat?"

"Well," Smith continued with less enthusiasm than before. "Scott Anderson came back with a jar of the serum the thralls use to keep the populace in line and I've been studying it. The results, I'm afraid, are quite worrying. The mix they use is particularly strong, as we all can testify, but it's the mix itself that concerns me."

Smith paused to take a drink of water. "The drugs used combine two different areas in medical science. The drug controlling the physical motor responses and the one inhibiting the mental commands from the synapses in the brain are counterproductive."

Harrington frowned.

"Let me explain. Before the vampires came these drugs were used for different ailments. Violent mental patients needed high doses of these drugs to prevent them from harming themselves or others. As a result, they needed constant care because they would be unable to function themselves. On the other hand, a patient suffering from depression would need to be able to move about freely and function normally in their day-to-day life. The thralls needed elements of both of these drugs, but there wasn't one drug that fit the bill, so they combined them."

"Go on," Harrington urged.

"You see, these drugs were never meant to be used together because they work against each other in the brain. One allows freedom of movement, but not of thought; the other promotes the opposite. To combine these drugs, one would have to experiment for a long time to get the balance right, and responses would vary for each person. The thralls obviously didn't have the time or inclination to worry about this, so they made up a batch and tested it. The dose they decided on is of a much higher strength than is needed and is actually harmful to the people taking it."

"How harmful?" Crockett asked leaning forward.

"It's eventually fatal, I'm afraid."

There was an audible intake of breath around the table before a number of people started to shout questions. Harrington could see that Smith was unable to cope with the volume or the desperation of the questioners, so he slammed his hand on the table to bring order to the proceedings.

"Is there a time frame for this kind of damage?" he asked when the noise had quieted sufficiently.

Smith caught the question as one would a lifeline. "Yes, there is. Now you must understand that this will be different for everyone—"

"Pat, just tell us," Harrington prompted.

"About 2 years."

A gasp rippled around the table.

"I believe that problems will occur in children first because they are less developed. They will develop severe headaches and, a short time later, they will begin to bleed from the ears. This will probably be followed within days by death. The elderly will probably follow, and then the rest of the population."

"But it's been nearly two years since the vampires took over," Crockett said unnecessarily.

"Yes, it has most probably already started."

CHAPTER
TWENTY– ONE

T he figure hunkered down and scooped up black ash from the ground. He glanced around the square and absently let it pass through his fingers. Dusk was approaching fast and shadows were lengthening around the burnt and broken buildings. The burnt out husk of the helicopter lay buried in the side of an abandoned building to the far west of the square, its tail rotor sticking straight up into the air as if proclaiming defiance. The figure smiled at the destruction around him. His eyes moved constantly, their dull grey colour perfectly complimenting both his personality and name.

"Steele."

The figure turned in answer and watched Nero approach.

"Up a bit early, aren't you?" Steele indicated the fading light from the sun.

"After the centuries I've lived," the vampire replied, "I've developed immunity to all but strong, direct light."

"Looks like quite a party you had here, Nero," Steele commented.

"Do not mistake my patronage for familiarity, human." Nero sneered, his voice undercut with a hard edge. "We have been made fools of and I do not care for such flippancy. I have brought you here because you have proved successful in the past. Your continued existence is wholly dependent on that continuing success."

Steele looked hard at the Vampire Lord and betrayed neither remorse nor fear. He hadn't survived the last two years by giving into these creatures, but he did have to be careful not to go too far. From the beginning he had proven himself more valuable to his masters when in control of his senses than as a helpless zombie. Steele had recognised the signs of defeat early on in the war and began to make plans to ensure his survival in the aftermath.

Steele was most comfortable when he was alone. Relationships had always been hard for him. An abusive father and alcoholic mother certainly hadn't helped, and he had finally run away at thirteen. He had lived on the streets, drifting from one end of the country to the other, sometimes working, sometimes stealing what he needed to survive. Five years he had wandered aimlessly, getting involved in more serious crimes as he got older and made contacts in the more lucrative end of the market. For the first time in his life, he had money and soon learned that money meant power. He liked power because it allowed him to make his own rules.

His luck had run out when he was eighteen. An armed robbery had gone wrong. The guy with him panicked and shot an off-duty cop. There was no hiding for cop killers. None of his "friends" would touch him; and it wasn't long before they caught up with him. His lifestyle had given him a callousness and indifference to his fellow man that was immediately obvious and attractive to the men in suits who visited him in prison. They talked about National Security and the need for certain people for difficult jobs. Steele really didn't care; if it got him out of prison he'd go back and kill his father for them. They offered him a deal that he accepted. After three years of incredible training he was a very dangerous man indeed.

Once the war had started they used him again and again to infiltrate the vampire nests and kill the main leaders. He ensured that confusion reigned in the covens and slowed the vampires' inexorable advances by promoting infighting and fearful uncertainty. It didn't take him long, however, to see that he was fighting a loosing battle. You just couldn't win a war that used your own dead against you. After a year of assassinating vampires, Steele simply changed sides. He beheaded the general in charge of his division and walked into the nearest vampire nest with his offering. The severed head intrigued the vampire patrol leader he came across enough to get him safe passage to the coven leader where he laid out his resume.

Steele suddenly shrugged and turned away with a smile. "Okay, boss, what do you want me to do?" he asked of the vampire.

"I want this cell of resistance found and crushed. You can have whatever you need, resources, men, anything."

"Are these the same guys who kicked your ass last month?" Steele asked innocently.

The look Nero gave him was beyond withering, and he wondered briefly if he had finally gone too far. He was surprised to note that he almost wished he had. The last few years had made him tired and lately he had begun to yearn for something, he wasn't sure what, but he felt empty inside. No, it was more that. He felt incomplete. This sort of thing had never happened to him before. Whatever it was, he didn't like how it felt. He was aware of pushing his masters that little bit further of late, but couldn't really bring himself to care.

"You tread a very thin line, human. I hope that you are still smiling at the completion of this mission. If you fail, believe me, I will enjoy watching you beg for death." With that, Nero stormed off and quickly disappeared in to the growing darkness.

Steele watched him go impassively.

"Are you sure?" Dan Harrington asked incredulously.

"Unfortunately, yes," Pat Smith replied. "It will have wildly varying time frames depending on people's metabolisms but, basically, the end result will be the same."

"Is there a cure?" Crockett asked.

"I'm afraid the only way to reduce the build-up of these chemicals in the brain is to stop taking them. Then, over time, the body will erode the excess."

The committee was stunned. Silence reigned as people just looked at each other, not quite knowing what they should say. Sandra felt tears in the corner of her eyes when she thought of all the children and their terrible fate.

"Well, at least it answers your question." Father Reilly broke the silence. Sandra turned to him, relieved to have a new focus. He addressed his comment directly to her father. "You were looking for a goal, something to strive for in the face of our changed circumstances. I believe we have one."

"What I said at the beginning of this meeting still stands: the thralls will be ready next time ..."

"Dan," Reilly interrupted, "children are going to start dying in agony any time now. We can't save everyone, but if we are going to sit here and let it happen, without at least trying to help those we can. Then what exactly are we fighting for?"

"With all due respect, Father," her father continued, "for all we know this could be the only free human community left. We must look at the bigger picture and the survival of the human race. We can't just throw lives away ..."

"Dad," Sandra saw him turn his attention toward her. "What would you do if I was still in there?" She knew that the harsh question pained him, but they couldn't just ignore this information.

"That's unfair, Sandra." She looked into her father's eyes. She had always seen him as a larger than life figure. Even in the time he wasn't around, she thought of him as aloof, unfazed by life's turmoil and steady as a rock against any adversity. As she looked into his eyes now she could see that the pressure of running the community and the decisions he had to make were taking their toll.

"I'm sorry," she stammered and turned her eyes from his, unable to bear the sadness she saw there any longer.

"Actually, I agree with Dan." Harris's voice was weak. Everyone leaned forward to hear. Sandra was surprised that support for her father had come from Harris. He tended to disagree with him as naturally as breathing.

"We can't continue as we have up to now. We'll be slaughtered." Harris paused to let his words sink in. "The element of surprise is gone, but that doesn't mean we have to sit here and do nothing. We must adapt, change our strategy. If they expect a frontal assault then we go in the back way. If they expect a small raid, then we attack in force—and the first thing we have to do is blow up the hospital where they produce the stuff."

Steele walked into the barracks and smiled at the frantic activity around him. Thralls rushed everywhere, attempting to repair damage to walls and equipment and get departments re-activated after the assault. He reached out and grabbed a passing thrall.

"Who's in charge around here?"

"General Evans, sir. He's over there," the thrall replied and indicated a large, heavy-set man supervising the erection of an office wall. Steele muttered an appreciative response and approached the General.

"General Evans, I presume." The general whirled with surprising speed for one so large and, after a second, his face registered recognition.

"So you're Steele," he stated. An infectious smile spread across his face. "Your reputation precedes you. Indeed, I've even seen some vampires act sheepish at the mention of your name. Welcome to hell."

Steele smiled, instantly liking this bear of a man. "Thank you, General."

"Oh, don't be so formal. It's Jack." The general thrust out his hand and enclosed Steele's in a vice-like grip. "I'm only a general since yesterday when Nero flew into a rage and disemboweled the entire ruling council. Between you and me," Evans looked from side to side conspiratorially, "I'll probably only be a general until his next ranting session, so make it quick."

Steele was shocked at this until he saw Evan's grin split even wider. "I think I'm going to enjoy working with you, Jack."

"What can I do for you?"

"Looks like a well orchestrated attack." Steele indicated the carnage surrounding them.

"Wasn't it just? You have to admire them don't you? They timed it well and even took out a tank before getting clean away. Not a trace, I believe." Evans laughed.

"You don't seem particularly worried," Steele observed.

"Well now, Steele, way I see it the vampires may own my body, but my soul still belongs to me. I will follow their orders, God help me, but I don't have to like them."

"That's pretty treasonous talk. I could get you executed for half of what you've just said."

"Yes, you could," Evans answered, "but I pride myself on the ability to judge a character from the get go, and I reckon I've judged you right. There's also the fact that I couldn't care less, of course."

The two men looked at each other for a long time. Steele knew the risk both of them were taking and recognised the force of will this man must have. Steele had argued when he had met the coven leader a year ago that making him a thrall would inhibit his effectiveness and ability to infiltrate human camps. The fact that he had been deep inside the Vampire territory before he had been found lent quite a lot of substance to this argument. He had succeeded in convincing the coven and had never been bound to a vampire, but he knew the level of control that the vampires could exert on their thralls. To even think those thoughts, let alone voice them, showed how strong this man's character was.

Finally, Steele nodded slightly and continued. "The supplies they took will only last them short term, so we can expect more attacks soon."

"No doubt. Any ideas on where they'll hit next."

"I've been thinking about that. I noticed from the report that they took a prisoner."

"Yes," Evans replied, "one of the technicians from the hospital, that's where they produce the ..."

"Serum," Steele finished. "Yes, I know."

CHAPTER
TWENTY–TWO

Scott Anderson and Ken Rodgers slipped quietly over the rubble and melted into the shadows of the city. They had been surprised that the hole left from their previous excursion had not been repaired. A board nailed to each jagged end of the wall was the only deterrent. Of course, the thralls were in a much higher state of awareness than ever before, but the three guards had been dispatched easily enough in the end.

The city was quiet; the cold evening air caused fog to rise from the water at the docks and gave a surreal look to the whole area.

"Looks like something out of an old horror movie." Rodgers grinned and Anderson threw his eyes up to heaven.

"I knew it was a mistake to bring you. Can't you take anything seriously?"

"Beer and women, after that I pretty much loose interest." Both men grinned this time.

Darkness had just fallen. The committee had decided that the thralls would probably expect a dawn attack. When the vampires were tucked up for the day, they'd be on higher alert. For that reason, they decided on an evening raid. While it was potentially more dangerous, they hoped that the thralls wouldn't expect a raid so late and the resulting confusion would make the chances of success better.

The two figures crept through the city and kept their eyes as much on the sky as on the streets. They moved slowly, their packs heavy with explosives, and had to change direction twice to avoid patrols. Five minutes from the hospital they heard a faint rustling in the air above them. Both men dived for cover when a vampire passed overhead. Sweat poured from the men as the creature passed mere feet above them and continued on, oblivious to their presence.

"I thought they had a great sense of smell, night vision and shit like that," Rodgers said. His relief was evident on his face.

"They do," Scott answered, "but luckily their arrogance gets the better of them. Most never really achieve their full potential. Come on, let's do this and get out of here."

Philip Warkowski was in hell. At least that was what it felt like. It was easier to identify those parts of his body that didn't hurt than those that did. He had awakened some five minutes ago and had been unable to move since. Each movement brought a fresh wave of nausea and pain, so he just lay there and tried to get his bearings. The room was dark and the only sign of life was the incessant pinging of the monitor by his bedside.

He tried to move his head. He knew he was in a hospital, but whose? Were thralls caring for him, so he could go on feeding their masters, or had someone brought him back to the Cave? Did Sarah and Jill make it out safely? Questions flooded his still muddled brain. The last thing he remembered was the explosion, and then half the city had fallen on him.

He gritted his teeth and slowly turned to his right, and an immediate rush of relief flooded through him. Sarah sat in the chair beside him, slumped in a half doze. There was no way that the thralls would let her stay with him. They both must be safe.

"Thank God," he muttered. His voice was low, but was so out of place in an otherwise quiet room that Sarah stirred and opened her eyes.

"Oh my God, you're awake," she exclaimed and rushed forward. She held his face and kissed him repeatedly.

"Aaagghhh!" He couldn't help but cry out as his body screamed in pain.

"Oh God, I'm sorry. That bloody serum wore off only this morning. I'm still a bit clumsy." She smiled delightedly, despite her obvious sincerity. Warkowski understood. He had walked around for a whole week with a permanent grin on his face when he first overcame the serum's effects.

"It's so good to see you, Sarah."

"God, but I've missed you, Phil," she answered. "They told me we were held for two years. We've missed our baby growing up." Tears sprang to her eyes and gently rolled down her cheeks.

"I know." Despite the pain, Warkowski reached his hand to her cheek. "But we're here now. We have the rest of our lives to make up for the past and look to the future. Speaking of Jill, how has she been affected by all this? Has she recovered?"

"Daddy, you're awake!"

The shrill scream came from the doorway. The child sprinted across the room and launched herself at the bed. Before either adult could stop her, she jumped up on the bed and wrapped her short, stubby arms around Warkowski and hugged with all her might. Tears flooded her eyes, too.

"I missed you," she said simply and buried her face in his chest.

Pains shot through every part of his body and consciousness began to slip away. He fought against the blackness to force his arms up and completely envelope his daughter's tiny body in his massive embrace. The pain still came in waves, but Warkowski hadn't been as happy as this in years. All the pain, the sacrifice and the work which had gotten him here melted away in that moment. He knew they would return, but it was enough for now.

"I missed you too, honey."

The two men slipped into the hospital through the same window that Scott had used before. At least this had been repaired. He briefly felt sorry for the poor maintenance guy before smashing the window again and entering the dark building.

"Okay, we'll be quicker if we split up. Set the charges every twenty feet or so on the far side of the building. We'll meet up back here in..." Anderson paused to look at his watch, "...say, twenty-five minutes."

Rodgers nodded and trotted off down the corridor, his pack bouncing from side to side as he went. He stopped at the end of the corridor to set the timer on an explosive, and then he rose and moved on to the next target area around the corner.

Scott had already laid most of his charges when a thrall came through a fire door right in front of him. He froze. His heart beat furiously in his chest, a cold sweat broke out down his back, and his muscles tensed. The thrall was distracted, reading a paper on a clipboard, and never saw the figure launch itself at him. The knife slid easily through the flesh under his chin, and the thrall collapsed into his arms, already dead.

Scott let the body fall to the ground. With only seven minutes left on the timer it was irrelevant whether the body was found or not. Three minutes later he met up with Rodgers again. They exited through the same window and hurried back the way they had come. When they were just outside the hospital grounds the explosions started. Both men grinned when the night lit up.

"Let's get out of here," Scott shouted above the roar of the explosions. "We can use the confusion to cover our tracks."

It took them an hour and a half to sneak back to the Cave. Both men looked exhausted from the trip and the stress of the night raid. The constant threat of discovery by thralls—or even worse, by vampires—had taken its toll and they almost fell through the door when they dialled in the code.

A hundred yards out from the house a figure watched from the crook of a tree. The night goggles he used gave him a clear picture of the entryway and the two men. He leaned back and smiled, his grey eyes twinkling in the pale light from the moon.

"Gotcha!"

CHAPTER
TWENTY-THREE

"Harris," the words were high pitched with an edge of panic, "you better come quickly." Scott Anderson gesticulated madly to attract his attention. Peter Harris looked up and frowned. Scott wasn't usually prone to panic. He excused himself from the conversation and headed over to him.

"What's up?"

"You'll have to see for yourself. Besides it's not something I want to say here." Anderson shoved Harris through the door toward the stairs.

"But Scott ..." Harris began, but Anderson had already sprinted up the stairs ahead of him and disappeared through the balcony exit. Harris shrugged and trotted up after him, muttering all the time about boiling oil and certain body parts.

The balcony was a small wooden deck area connected to the second level of the upper house and gave a good view of the surrounding approach to the facility. Harris began to feel worried when he noticed that John Kelly was already there, his attention riveted to the East and binoculars clasped tightly to his eyes.

"Peter," Kelly's face was white, "you better take a look."

Harris took the binoculars to look in the indicated direction. "Oh, Shit," he said. What looked like the entire thrall army were setting up camp about three hundred yards from the house.

"They...they must have followed me last night." Anderson's face was ashen. He couldn't quite raise his eyes from the floor. "God. I'm sorry. It's all my fault."

"Scott," Harris put his hand on the man's shoulder, "we'll probably never know for sure how they found out. Regardless, we have to deal with it now, so don't fall apart on me." He turned to Kelly. "Don't start a panic, but get everyone down to the Cave. Tell Reiss and Rodgers to join me here, and you'd better get Crockett. This is more his territory." Harris rattled off the orders. "His idea of flooding the area seems to have worked."

Crockett arrived and Harris indicated the growing build up of thralls. The two men saw the three tanks for the first time. All of them were stuck fast and listed forward, making use of their heavy guns impossible. Two dozen thralls pushed, pulled and heaved on lines without luck.

"Come on, they're sure to try an assault soon. Let's get moving."

The creature that had been Jack Walton woke. He could smell blood and his stomach ached. He rose fluidly from the bed and looked around at the two other beds in the room. Only one was occupied and, with a lick of his lips, he approached the other occupant. He looked down at Henshaw's sleeping figure and smiled. Without a moment's hesitation he tore the man's throat out and blood poured into his mouth. Henshaw woke briefly and saw the creature's hellish face. The drugs he'd been given held the pain at bay, but also made his muscles sluggish, so he managed only a soft gurgling noise before he drowned in his own blood.

The creature swallowed and felt a surge of power course through him. His senses tingled with the hot fluid.

"Breakfast in bed," he cackled and moved on to the next room. The door was closed, but the creature could hear the high-pitched giggling of a young girl in the next room.

Young flesh, it thought and its mouth watered at the prospect. The creature reveled in its newfound power and didn't bother to check if the door was locked or not. Instead it just crashed straight through.

"Report!" General Evans barked the order at his Lieutenant.

"Sir, we've set up a perimeter around the facility. Nothing can get out." The Lieutenant panted while he recovered from his exertions.

"Having a spot of bother?" Evans asked and indicated the hive of activity around the tanks.

"Oh…yes, sir. The entire approach to the house is flooded. The tanks sank on us." The Lieutenant sounded embarrassed.

And well he might, thought Evans.

"I've already radioed back to base to send up the long range artillery to flush them out." The Lieutenant brightened, as if this news would make up for his mistake.

"That's mighty efficient of you," Evans commented with a sneer.

The sarcasm was lost on the Lieutenant, who grinned like a puppy and said, "Thank you, sir. I've also given the order for a frontal assault …"

"You've what?"

The Lieutenant cowered from the volume of the General's outburst.

Evans reigned in his anger before he continued. "Son, don't you think that if these folks went to all that trouble to flood this entire area, they might have a few more surprises waiting for some idiot who walks up to the front door?"

"I'm sorry, sir, I didn't think …"

"No, I don't suppose you did." Evans threw his eyes up to heaven. Both men turned then to the sound of gunfire and men screaming. "Come on, Lieutenant; let's see what we can salvage from this mess."

The door burst open in a shower of splinters, and Jill screamed when the creature appeared in the doorway. Sarah pushed the child behind her and backed away. The creature moved like a blur to cut off their retreat. A deep rattle erupted from its throat. The creature was well over six foot; a vicious tangle of teeth dominating its features. The rattle, Sarah realised, was laughter. The hairs of her neck bristled when the creature approached.

"Get away from them, you son of a bitch."

The vampire whirled and tensed its muscles for an attack. Warkowski managed to pull himself from the bed, but was still using it for support.

The deep rattle came again. "You have got to be kidding, human." The vampire laughed and purposely turned again to Sarah and Jill.

The roar began deep in the pit of his stomach; Warkowski was halfway across the room before it erupted from his throat. The creature barely had time to turn before Warkowski tackled him and sent the two of them crashing against the wall.

With strength born of despair, fuelled by a passionate love for his family, Warkowski laid into the creature and showered blow after blow into its demonic face. Muscles tore, bones crunched and sutures ripped, but he continued to assault the creature. Blood began to pour from reopened wounds at Warkowski's side, but he ignored it all. The speed of his attack caught the vampire unprepared and, caught in the middle of a transformation, the relentless, vicious blows kept it off balance. Its flesh still rippled over bone as it tried to complete the change.

Adrenaline pumped through Warkowski's body and dulled the pain while he pummelled the creature. The vampire's wickedly sharp talons flayed wildly around him, but he was unable to aim or take the initiative as blow after blow connected with its head. The vampire fell back further. Suddenly it tripped over some furniture, fell heavily to the ground, and crushed a chair in the process.

Warkowski didn't miss a beat. He straddled the creature and continued pummeling him. "Let me hear you laugh now, motherfucker," he panted, each word punctuated by another blow. Warkowski gulped in air and finally paused in his assault. His arms felt like lead weights; he couldn't go on. The vampire was already recovering, so he looked frantically around for a weapon. Suddenly he saw the shattered chair. He wrenched one of the legs from the broken frame, but the vampire was already finishing its transformation.

Warkowski blanched when he looked down at the creature beneath him. Red eyes glowed balefully up at him in a face that was more wolf than human. Long, course hair covered its features; an extended snout replaced the mouth and nose. Long canine teeth sprouted from the upper jaws, and its breath reeked of death and decay. The creature shot its arms up and grabbed Warkowski by the throat.

"I will enjoy eating the little girl most of all. Young flesh is so much more tender." The creature's mouth was not designed for speech, but the general meaning was all too clear.

Warkowski couldn't breathe. The creature's claws were like vice grips around his throat. His vision began to fade. With one last, desperate effort Warkowski gripped the chair leg in his hand and brought it down on the creature with all his remaining strength. The wood passed easily through the creature's chest and its eyes flew wide at this unexpected turn of events. For a second it looked as if were about to speak, and then Warkowski leaned forward on the chair leg and drove it further into the creature's heart. The red eyes dimmed and the creature died with no more than a whimper.

"See?" Warkowski pulled himself to his feet and gripped a nearby table for support. "A piece of cake." He managed a smile before he collapsed into his wife's arms, and then everything went black.

Rodgers skidded to a halt just inside the room and took in the scene in front of him. "Jesus, are you okay in here?"

Sarah Warkowski knelt on the floor with her husband's head cradled in her lap. Her daughter, Jill, stood just in front, as if standing guard over them both.

"We are now," she smiled and caressed her husband's cheek.

Rodgers approached the steaming pool in the corner. "Did he do that?" he asked.

"Yes, he did."

"How?" Rodgers stammered. "He could barely move last I saw him."

"It threatened us," Sarah said simply, as if that was explanation enough.

"Jesus," Rodgers repeated. "I'll see if I can get someone to help you patch him up."

Harris stood on the balcony and watched the thralls' approach. "Must be at least thirty of them," he commented to Dan Reiss and Scott Anderson.

Before either of them could reply, Rodgers raced through the door. "Sorry," he panted. "Jesus, you'll never believe what I just saw. Warkowski's awake—"

"Thank God," Harris sighed.

"No, that's not it. You remember Walton? Tall fellow, he was on the last assault?"

Harris nodded.

"Well," Rodgers continued, "he must have been bitten during the attack. He just turned all vamp and tried to attack Warkowski's family."

"Are they all right?"

"Yeah, Warkowski beat the shit out of him with his bare hands. Fuck, I wouldn't want to be on the wrong side of that guy. What's up here?" he finished as if he just remembered why he had come to the balcony in the first place.

"They've found us," Harris replied

"Oh shit."

"Crockett and his men are in position," Dan Harrington reported when he came up behind Rodgers.

"That's great, Dan, thanks." Harris turned to the others. "Okay, it's time to kick some ass."

CHAPTER
TWENTY-FOUR

C aptain Pierce led his team toward the house. Twenty-nine men spread out to either side of him, armed with a vast array of weaponry. The ruling thralls had tried many times to make the militia into an army, insisting on uniforms and similar weaponry. Unfortunately, with so many weapons available in this New World, the thralls ignored the dictates. They each continued to carry those weapons that were more suited their personalities.

The uniforms started out the same, but while they still retained a similar look, these too had been adapted. The ruling council had all but given up on disciplining these transgressions when the vampires had cleaned house and the next level had taken over. Up till now the new council had been too busy to address this issue. The ranks had taken advantage and openly carried such diverse weaponry as bazookas and chain-fed machine guns.

The main downside to this was that the thralls never really acted as a cohesive team. Even now Pierce could see the outside edges of the ranks overtaking his own lead position. They looked more like a group out on maneuvers than a platoon about to go into battle.

Dawn had come and gone, but a slight mist still licked at the river's surface and the edges of the nearby forest. There was no sign of life from the house. He whistled and signaled for the outer edges to take up positions on either side of the complex. Their approach was confident; all the thralls walked upright, rather than sprinting in a crouch to present a smaller target.

Even if they're here, they're only humans, Pierce thought.

He heard a click and stopped dead. He looked down at the thin metal line that lay on the ground under his boot. His eyes flicked from side to side and he noticed that the line ran up to a small clump of earth beside him. He saw also that many of these mounds surrounded the entire approach.

"Oh, shit!"

And then the Claymore mines exploded.

Thousands of small metal bearings shot from the mines at ferocious speeds. Projectiles filled the area in front of the house; they shredded flesh and shattered bones. Bodies jerked spasmodically in a grotesque dance as the platoon was hit repeatedly by the flying shrapnel. Some of the thralls managed to get a few rounds off, firing blindly, before they were hit by the hail of death. The carnage was terrible; blood flowed copiously and turned the whole area red. Some of the bodies fell into the river, and red swirls eddied along with the current while bodies floated by the bank.

When the smoke cleared the grounds were littered with bodies and limbs. There wasn't a sound. The Lieutenant, ashen-faced, turned to Evans and swallowed deeply. "Should I call off the second platoon, Sir?"

"What second platoon?" Evans shouted.

The second Platoon had just settled into position when they heard the explosions and the screaming. From their location in the forest, behind and to the east of the complex, they couldn't see what was happening and had no way of knowing who was screaming.

"Sounds like Alpha platoon is really giving 'em hell, sir."

Captain Gilbert heard the words coming from his Sergeant's mouth, but he had to shake his head to bring himself back into focus. "What's that, Jim?" he said.

"I was just saying I hope they leave something for us, sir."

Peter Gilbert nodded and prepared to launch his own attack. A loud squawk from the radio delayed his order and he looked to the communications officer for news.

"Sir, command has called off the attack. We're to wait for the artillery."

"Oh, shit," the sergeant cursed. "We miss out on all the action."

Gilbert nodded agreement. "Maybe next time," he consoled and the men began to back up from the fringe of the trees.

Just then the whole forest seemed to come alive. Branches that had been held taught by strong rope were suddenly cut, and the whiplash sent the limbs shooting toward the platoon. The thralls at the rear of the column were the first to notice anything. The rustling of the tress increased in volume until the first branches crashed through the clearing and smashed into the retreating soldiers.

The thralls were picked up off the ground and flung violently against the surrounding trees. Bodies were wrapped brutally around tree trunks, bones were snapped and crushed when they dropped to the ground. The other thralls panicked and began to run in all directions. Two of them ran out toward the complex. A solid wooden frame suddenly appeared from above and slammed into the fleeing thralls. The frame was liberally dotted with long, wickedly sharp spikes that impaled the thralls with such speed they didn't have time to scream. Three others ran toward the river and the ground suddenly dropped from beneath them. They disappeared from view, and then the screaming began when they landed on the stakes set into the base of the hole.

Gilbert tried to regain control by shouting orders, but the screaming from the injured and the panicked shouting of those trying to escape drowned out his commands. He pulled his M-16 from around his back and fired three rounds into the air. The sudden crack of the gun was so out of place in the forest that most of the platoon stopped and looked to the sound.

"Okay, let's get out of here, but carefully…"

Before he had a chance to speak further, there were a number of explosions around them. Everyone looked frantically around to see what this latest trap might be.

The trees began to fall; there seemed to be hundreds of them. The noise was thunderous, like standing under a waterfall. The trees fell, taking smaller trees and branches with them when they dropped toward the platoon. Some of the thralls stared, frozen in fear, while the trunks loomed larger. Others bolted aimlessly, only to be hit by stray branches or crushed by the falling trunks. Thralls were crushed or impaled by the wood when the trees crashed to earth and completely decimated the entire area.

After the last tree had fallen, the only sound to come from the clearing was the occasional creaking of wood. From the pit, at the edge of the clearing, the radio, which had miraculously survived, squawked to life and demanded attention.

"No answer, sir." The communications officer shook his head to emphasise the point, and the Lieutenant turned to Evans.

"I heard," Evans muttered and saved the Lieutenant the embarrassment.

"At least the artillery will be here within the hour. We'll get them then." The Lieutenant was ashen faced and didn't really look as if he had convinced himself, let alone his stone-faced General.

Steele arrived at the scene around mid-afternoon. By that time tents had been erected and cooking fires lit. Steele sauntered into camp, where the smell of roasted meat filled the air. Thralls stood miserably around, like drunks at closing time. Bodies littered the lawn in front of the house and added to the overall pall of despair that had descended over the camp.

Steele whistled while he looked about him and then made his way over to Evans.

"I see you found them, then. Come to admire your handiwork, eh?" Evans indicated the complex.

Steele reeled, pretending he'd been shot. "General, you wound me." Steele sobered and looked directly at the General. "Actually, you're half right. Yes, I did find them; but no, I didn't report it."

"What...how?" Evans stammered.

"Looks like I don't enjoy the lofty level of trust I thought, huh?" Steele smiled while he spoke.

"You might be right. You don't look too worried about it, though."

"Worry is for those with something to loose, General." Steele dropped his gaze. "Still, it looks as though our friends are doing quite well."

Evans followed Steele's gaze to the complex.

"Yes, they haven't fired a shot yet, but they've taken out fifty of my men."

Both men were distracted by the noises of heavy machinery and looked over to see the artillery beginning to arrive.

"You don't seem too worried about that, General," Steele countered. "It's a pity those guns will pound the shit out of them, isn't it? Doesn't seem quite sporting, eh?"

"Well, if you'll excuse me, I have things to do." Evans strode purposely away.

In the middle of bustling activity, General Jack Evans stood still, impassive and outwardly calm. But inside turmoil raged. All around him thralls hurried about their business. The walls surrounding the house had already been cleared to make way for the large guns, and the thralls busied themselves un-coupling equipment, rolling artillery into position, checking sights and unloading ammunition.

The young Lieutenant shouted orders. Evans could tell that it would not be long before the human facility was a smouldering ruin. He looked down at the grenade in his hands, focused his will on the pin, and sent an impulse to his hand to pull it. For the fourth time in the last few minutes his finger didn't move.

Goddamn mind control, he thought bitterly.

Over the last two years Evans had pushed against the control that bound him to the Vampires. He still snapped to orders when a master was in sight. Their very presence somehow acted as a stimulant, but during the day he had been able to push his independence further and further. He had gotten to a stage now where he could think relatively freely and perform small actions of defiance. He had even been able to delay the order to reinforce the thralls during the last assault to give the rebels needed time to get away.

He had also succeeded in coming to the artillery base; even to liberate the grenade, but he just couldn't pull the damn pin.

"Come on it's only half an inch," he muttered. Sweat poured from his forehead. He looked up and saw that the thralls were nearly ready to commence firing and he tried once more. He put every ounce of will power into moving the pin.

"Those pins can be a bitch sometimes," a voice whispered in his ear. His heart leapt in his chest and, dizzy with the shock, he turned slowly to see Steele's grinning face. "I had a think about what you said."

Evans could barely hear Steele for the blood pounding in his head. The two men stood mere feet apart and looked at each other while activities continued around them. Finally, Evans saw Steele reach over and take the grenade. He was powerless to stop him.

"And?"

"I think they deserve a chance, don't you?" Evans said.

Evans watched Steele closely and saw him nod slightly. Then without another word Steele pulled the pin. The metal clasp sprang free and he dropped the explosive into a nearby ammunition crate.

"Run," he said.

Evans didn't need to be told twice.

The Lieutenant noticed the two men talking, but paid little attention while he readied his crew for the barrage. He smiled in anticipation when the first shell was loaded into the breach. He raised his hand to signal the firing order when he noticed the General break into a run out of the corner of his eye. He turned slightly and frowned at this strange turn of events.

"General ..." he began, and then the grenade exploded.

It took only a fraction of a second more before the rest of the ammunition followed suit. The roar was deafening.

Evans and Steele launched themselves to the ground and covered their heads while shrapnel and rock flew in every direction. Bodies were shredded and equipment launched into the air by the force of the blast, only to land in twisted, useless piles across the lawn.

"Whoooooaaaaaa!" Steele shouted. "What a rush! Come on, let's see what other mischief we can create."

Jack Evans pulled himself to his feet and looked up at the darkening sky. "It'll be nightfall soon," he commented with a worried frown.

"Yeah, oh well, you only live once," Steele replied simply.

CHAPTER
TWENTY-FIVE

The lawn surrounding the area where the artillery had been set up was completely scorched. Small fires licked hungrily at any combustible material; wood, clothes, flesh and rubber all burnt. A thick pall of smoke drifted lazily across the lawn. The silence was broken by the thunder of feet as thralls from the lower camp rushed over to put out fires and tend the wounded and dying.

Thralls gagged on the fumes. They went from fire to fire, and the dense spray of the extinguishing fluid only added to the confusion. Sergeant Philips looked around at the carnage and shook his head. This whole campaign had been a complete mess; bad preparation and equally bad leadership had already led to too many deaths.

Just then a shout came from his left. He could barely see the two thralls through the mist, but they seemed to struggle with a third figure, so he hurried over. When he got closer he heard the soldiers urge the figure they held on the ground to stay still until the medical team arrived to check his wounds.

The person on the ground pushed the thralls away and rose with a bellow. "Get away from me, you incompetent bastards!" the Lieutenant screamed. His face was burnt red and ragged pieces of flesh hung from his cheeks. Black soot covered his body, a stark contrast to the wild, white eyes that bored straight into the Sergeant's face. "Where is he?" he screamed.

"Who?" Philips held his hands up to try to placate his superior.

"General-fucking-Evans, that's who."

"Sir," Philips began calmly, "I haven't seen the General. What happened here?"

"I'll tell you what happened, that bastard threw a grenade into the ammunition dump. He did this!" He waved around him to indicate the carnage. "The traitorous bastard, I want him found, Sergeant."

The news hit Philips like a brick. *The General was a traitor?* He was shocked. He had thought that nothing could surprise him much anymore, but he couldn't really see the General as a traitor. Until he could confirm one way or the other whether this was true, though, he decided to play along and report to the Lieutenant.

Philips turned to the two thralls who had found the Lieutenant and issued orders. The two soldiers registered shock on their faces, but turned and began to gather up a few more recruits. Then they disappeared into the mist.

"What do we do about the humans, sir?" Philips asked.

The Lieutenant's face registered pure hatred. "Kill them, Sergeant. Kill every fucking one of them."

"What happening out there?" Rodgers scratched his head while he watched the explosions rip through the artillery.

"I don't know," Harris replied, "but I sure am glad we're not the ones on the receiving end."

"Amen to that."

The two men on the balcony watched the late afternoon light up with explosive reports that shattered the tranquil countryside. Everything had gone perfectly so far. They had watched grimly while the thralls were decimated on the lawn, and then listened to the screams from those in the forest. Neither man took pleasure from the slaughter. This is war, as Dan Harrington had said, and shit happens.

Crockett came through the doorway and asked, "What's all the commotion?"

"The artillery dump just blew up," Harris replied and turned to Crockett with a broad grin.

"Get the fuck out of here," Crockett exclaimed incredulously.

"It's true," Rodgers cut in, "took all the guns with it."

"God, that's a relief. I really didn't want to give up the upper floors that easily."

"Why not? Why don't we batten down the hatches and get below ground? It'll take a tank to pull those doors down." Rodgers voiced the question that many of the men secreted in positions around the house had thought about over the last hour.

"The Cave is our last resort," Crockett explained. "Once we go down there, that's it, we've nowhere else to go. At least up here we still have options, few though they might be. As for the doors, well, I doubt they'll hold out long against the vampires when they arrive."

"Oh yeah, I nearly forgot about them." Rodgers looked earnestly at the other two. "Listen, I really don't want to go back to the way we were…"

"Don't worry, we've seen to that," Harris interrupted. He grimly placed a hand on Rodgers' shoulder. "No one is going back to that life. One way or another, it ends tonight. Now, if you'll excuse me, I have a certain lady to see before they attack." Harris turned toward the door.

"What makes you think they'll attack now? Won't they wait for the vampires?" Crockett asked.

"Don't think so. Take a look out there." Harris handed the binoculars to Crockett and the worthy looked eagerly out over the grounds.

"I see what you mean." The entire approach to the complex was covered with thralls. Standing three deep the line stretched from the river right across to the forest. "Kind of reminds you of *Zulu*, doesn't it?" Crockett commented.

"What?" asked Rodgers.

"Rourke's Drift," Harris answered when he saw Rodgers blank face. "A small party of English soldiers defended an outpost in Africa in the 1800s against thousands of Zulu warriors."

"Oh," replied Rodgers. "Did they make it?"

"As a matter of fact, yes, some did."

"Some? How many is some?" Rodgers asked, but Harris had already gone.

Sergeant Philips looked down along the line of men. Some two hundred thralls had gathered just out of range of the complex. The Lieutenant's orders demanded a full assault; no feints and no patrols like the last time. This time they were going to throw everything they had at them and level the place.

"Bazooka!" he called. Two men pushed their way to the front of the line and knelt while they took aim at the doors to the house.

Philips turned to his Lieutenant. "Sir, we're ready when you are."

"Thank you, Sergeant. Have you detained General Evans yet?"

"Not yet, Sir. I have a patrol out looking for him."

"Very well, commence the attack."

The two rockets shot across the lawn and left a fine smoke trail in their wake. They impacted simultaneously and the explosions rocked the entire building. The doors disintegrated. Wood and masonry flew in every direction as the entrance, and most of the surrounding supports blew apart.

The Lieutenant grinned when he saw the destruction. A jagged hole measuring some twenty feet in diameter and ten feet in height became visible when the evening breeze whisked the smoke into the darkening sky.

"Sergeant!" he shouted. "Advance."

Harris saw the men with bazookas kneel and take aim from his vantage point on the balcony. "Incoming!" he shouted and ran into the house to take cover.

The explosion was huge. Harris was thrown across the upstairs landing and sprawled into a bedroom wall. Splinters and rock fragments flew everywhere in a deadly hail. Harris rolled into a ball and covered his head in a vain attempt to protect himself.

He heard a few screams from downstairs, but didn't have time to check the extent of people's injuries. He brought his weapon to bear and waited for the thralls to arrive.

Rodgers picked himself up from behind the sofa on the ground floor, and then quickly dived back down when bullets ripped the furniture to shreds. He had been on the first floor, directly in front of the doors, when the blast had come. The force of the explosion had been so great that he had been lifted up and thrown through the banister railing. He had landed directly in the path of the thralls, so he remained behind the sofa to protect himself while they swarmed through the ruined entrance.

The noise was deafening. Bullets gauged holes in the stone fireplace behind him, and splinters of stone covered his prone form. He pulled himself along by his elbows and returned fire blindly around the far end of the couch. Gunfire erupted from above him and men poured fire down in support.

Harris ran from one side of the landing to the other and tried vainly to outrun a line of bullets rapidly catching up to him. He had to move from his previous position when the thralls had lobbed a grenade that bounced across the wooden floor to lie ten feet from where he had crouched. Too close to stay and too far to get to it and kick it out of reach. He launched himself up and ran the only direction left to him, straight into the thralls' line of fire.

He neared the end of the landing and jumped, then rolled into a kneeling position and brought his machine gun to bear, letting loose a sustained burst of fire. This unexpected development caught the thralls by surprise and their bodies twitched while round after round hit home.

More thralls appeared through the hole while Harris changed his magazine and looked for cover. The noise was incredible. Some fifteen men in various positions around the house and an unknown number of thralls all fired and screamed in the close confines. Explosions erupted everywhere. Both sides threw grenades and added to the chaos. The structure of the house was a complete mess. Thralls now poured into the house through windows and the other gaping holes that had been blown through the downstairs walls.

Bodies lay piled on top of each other. Harris' men poured a viscous hail of fire at these entrances. Thralls were decimated one by one while they poured through the breach, but it wasn't all one-sided. Harris could see many of his own men already dead. Pools of blood seeped into the carpet or pooled on the wooden floors where they lay. Others slumped against walls, their shattered limbs held uselessly to their sides.

And all the time the thralls kept coming.

Rodgers heard the window to his left shatter and he looked up in time to see a thrall point his gun straight at him. With no time to think, Rodgers rolled out of the way of this new threat as bullets tore up the floor where he had lain. Unfortunately, the only space open to him was the open floor. He found himself on his back looking up at four very surprised thralls.

"Surprise," Rodgers grinned and then pulled the trigger. The thralls were so close to the weapon that the bullets literally ripped through them and lifted the bodies into the air. Blood spattered everywhere and the warm liquid splashed across Rodgers' face. With no time to clear the blood, he jumped to his feet and made a break for the stairs, dodging both enemy and friendly fire on his way. The thrall at the window was now inside and already others had begun to join him.

"Shit!" he muttered. He picked up speed while the thralls gave chase.

Thralls were already on the stairs when Rodgers hit the bottom of the steps at a run. They were not expecting an attack from behind, and he poured fire into them without missing a step. He sprinted past them as bullets flew past his head and picked at his clothes.

"Stop firing, you blind bastards!" he screamed. "Good guy coming through!" and he launched himself flat on the landing as the men ahead of him sent a hail of fire into the thralls chasing close behind.

CHAPTER
TWENTY-SIX

D an Reiss knelt beside Bill Anderson as they poured round after round into the hall below. Bazooka fire and grenades had torn further holes in the structure, and thralls poured into the house. Their sheer number was overwhelming. No matter how many the men killed, more appeared in their place. The stairs were littered with the bodies of the dead and wounded. The carnage delayed the thralls' advance as they climbed over the bodies.

Dan saw men crouched in doorways along the hall. They kept the thralls pinned down while they dodged out, fired and dodged back into the rooms before the thralls could respond. Most of the fire was blind; bullets flew everywhere. People on both sides died or grunted in pain when ricochets embedded themselves in flesh and furniture at impossible angles.

Grenades flew from side to side. With the thralls so closely packed, every grenade explosion among them took a terrible toll. Blood flowed down the wooded steps and body after body fell while the humans defended the stairwell. Despite the carnage; despite the death, the thralls kept coming. Reiss could understand their single mindedness. Like the humans, they too feared their masters and would surely pay dearly for failure.

Slowly, inexorably, they forced the humans back.

Bill Anderson screamed as a line of bullets stitched across his chest. The force of the impact threw him backward. Reiss glanced quickly at his colleague and saw the damage to his chest. He knew immediately he could do nothing to save him. The sheer volume of fire forced him to retreat further down the hall, while bullets flew around him and drove splinters of wood and masonry into his flesh.

He heard a scream behind him and glanced back in time to see Scott Anderson launch himself to his feet and run down the landing toward the thralls. He screamed at the top of his lungs for his fallen brother, his rage evident in his face while he ran. The gun bucked wildly in his hands as he ploughed into the first line of thralls.

The blood-spattered vision coming toward them took the thralls completely by surprise. They panicked and tried to retreat back the way they had come. Unfortunately for them, too many others were pushing from behind. Anderson caught them from his end and strafed his weapon from side to side while he screamed his grief. The front line of thralls dropped, but the second line pushed past and returned fire. Reiss was torn. Running after Anderson was suicide, but he couldn't just stay here and do nothing.

Under cover of the confusion from Anderson's mad sprint he started forward again. He regained his position beside the still form of Bill Anderson to provide covering fire. The stairway was a scene of utter confusion. The thralls had recovered from the initial shock and had already regrouped to advance again. On the top stair Scott screamed his rage and he pumped round after round into the advancing horde.

Tears welled up in Reiss' eyes when he saw Scott spin backward. A bullet ripped through his shoulder, and the force of the impact forced Scott to drop his weapon. For a second there was total silence, and then Scott turned again to the thralls. Unarmed, he stood defiantly at the top of the stairs when the thralls opened fire at point blank range. The sheer volume of fire tore him apart. He was already dead long before he slumped to the ground. The thralls gathered around the body and spat on it when they passed. Reiss could do nothing but use this distraction to retreat again down the corridor.

It had become impossible to see inside the upper floors of the house. The smoke from the explosions and small fires added to the gloom of the descending darkness. Harris fired at any flashes of light in the hall or shifting of shadows. He couldn't see any of his colleagues and dared not shout out to them in case he gave his position away.

Suddenly a dark shadow ran toward him and he brought up his gun to fire only to ease off the trigger at the last minute. "Nearly blew your fool head off," he chastised Rodgers when he came level. "It's just as well I recognised that stupid grin of yours."

"You'd probably have missed anyway the way you shoot." Rodgers tried to grin, but the enthusiasm just wasn't there. Too many friends lay dead on this landing and he could hear others scream for help where they lay in the gloom. "How many are left?" he asked.

"No idea," grunted Harris. "There's sporadic fire over there," he indicated the far end of the landing, "but other than that I don't hear anyone." Harris rolled out into the hall and sent a burst of fire down the landing to keep the advancing thralls in check.

"Nearly dark," Rodgers commented, "they'll be here soon."

"Yea, let's hope we've bought them enough time."

"Do you really think we can win?" Rodgers asked.

"Probably not, but we'll take a few of these fuckers with us."

Dan Harrington stood at the Cave door and listened to the muffled sounds of battle through the large metal entrance. He leaned his forehead against the cool metal and cringed with every shot.

"We can't just sit here and wait, Dad." Sandra Harrington looked into her father's eyes.

"Crockett was adamant we keep this door closed no matter what we heard. If the thralls get in here it's all over." He looked around for support. "Father Reilly, you tell her." his eyes pleaded with the priest.

Reilly listened to the staccato bursts of gunfire and the occasional deep thump of explosions and sighed deeply, "Sandra," he began, "your father ..."

"No!" Sandra Harrington interrupted. "I don't accept that. How can letting them die possibly help us?" The tears began to roll down her cheeks, but her face was set in a determined manner. "We're in this together. Hiding here like frightened rabbits, even if we do survive, is no victory at all. I want no part of it."

The house was quiet. There hadn't been a shot for a full five minutes and both sides used the time to take stock. Muffled whispers were barely audible through the gloom. An occasional cough or splutter were the only audible sounds. Harris and Rodgers inched their way along the last few feet of the landing and looked for a way back down to the ground floor. They had run out of room on the landing and the next push from the thralls would overrun their position.

Dan Reiss nearly tripped over Vince Crockett when he retreated to the other wall of the far landing.

"Did you see anyone else?" Crockett asked.

"Afraid not."

Just then there was a sound of pounding feet on the landing as the thralls began the final push.

"Give me your gun," Crockett reached out for the weapon. "I'll cover you while you try and get downstairs."

"No way," Reiss protested, "we'll go together or—" Reiss looked down at Crockett and noticed his injuries for the first time. His shirt was soaked in blood and his left hand was clutched tightly against his stomach, holding his insides in place.

"Oh my God," Reiss exclaimed, "let me try—"

"No point, I can't move. Now get out of here before they reach us."

Reiss delayed another few seconds and wrestled with his conscience. The sudden eruption of gunfire from the stairs startled him into action, and he ran to the end of the landing while Crockett opened up and sprayed fire down the landing. Reiss heard Crockett scream abuse at the approaching thralls. After too short a time the screaming and the gunfire stopped.

Harris hung from the top floor landing while bullets tore into the wooden balustrades. Rodgers stood over him and pumped round after round into the advancing thralls. A bullet embedded itself in the wood under Harris' fingers and splinters ripped into his flesh. He screamed in pain, lost his grip and fell to the floor below.

His fall was cushioned by dead bodies. Blood splattered over him while he waded through the carnage. Above him Rodgers spun around from the force of a bullet and fell toward him, headfirst, his body limp. Harris rushed to break the man's fall. He launched himself at the falling figure and managed to get his arms around Rodgers and straighten his prone form so that he fell on his back and not his neck.

The thralls completed their sweep above and started firing over the balcony. Harris grabbed the unconscious Rodgers and pulled him to an alcove where he quickly examined him. A bullet had grazed his head. Blood oozed from the wound. Another had taken a chunk of flesh from the soft flesh of his upper arm on its way clean through. Harris tore his shirt and pressed the rag against the wound in an effort to stem the flow of blood.

Thralls now occupied the entire house and still they continued to pour in. Harris brought his weapon up with his free hand and heard the dull click when the hammer fell on an empty chamber.

Overhead he could hear the thunderous sound of wings.

The door, hidden in a recess under the stairs, opened and immediately shot a beacon of light through the dark. The sudden appearance of the light took many thralls by surprise, and the invading force had a small but important advantage when they pushed into the crowded hall. Harris saw the figure of Sandra Harrington burst through the light and open fire on the startled thralls. Harris grabbed Rodgers and made his way through the confusion to the open door.

Dan Reiss also saw the door open and felt renewed hope. He had landed heavily on the floor when he had tried to avoid the thralls, and now pain shot through his ankle when he put any weight on it. He steeled himself against the pain and limped toward the rescue party. His ankle gave way with a sickening crack and he fell again. He looked and saw the bone protruding at an awkward angle. He could go no further.

"Hang on," he heard. The closeness of the voice startled him and he instinctively brought his gun up.

"Don't be stupid," the voice continued, "if I wanted you dead you're not really in any position to stop me, now are you?"

Reiss didn't have a choice, so he allowed the stranger to approach. Before the figure swept him up and carried him to the door, he caught a glimpse of a stocky, solid build topped by grey hair. The thralls recovered quickly and had already forced the rescue party back with their superior numbers. Sandra looked around and spotted Harris slip behind the thralls and move to the Cave entrance.

"Are there any more?" she shouted over the gunfire. Harris shook his head and continued on into the Cave. "All right, people, let's wrap it up and get back inside," she shouted and the humans retreated under a blanket of fire.

Just as they were about to shut the door Sandra saw a figure struggling with a man over his shoulder.

"Hold it!" she ordered and reopened the door for the approaching figures. She stopped suddenly and barred the door when she noticed the uniform and brought the gun around to point directly at the thrall. "Just drop him and leave!" she barked.

The General eased the man off his shoulder and allowed the humans to take him inside.

"Why?" Sandra asked.

"There's been enough senseless killing, don't you think?"

Sandra Harrington nodded and went to close the door.

"Good luck," the stranger added.

"Thank you," she replied and then the door closed.

"Lieutenant, we have him," the sergeant reported happily when his men dragged the General before their new commander.

"Excellent," the Lieutenant replied "What about the humans?"

"We've cleared the house, about twenty dead, and the rest escaped into a hidden doorway. We are setting explosives now to gain entry."

"And our own losses?"

"Um, sir, we haven't had time to ascertain the full..."

"That many, Sergeant? No matter, you have done well." He looked up at the sound of wings in the night and saw three vampires peel off from the swarm and approach them while the rest continued on to the house.

"Bring the traitor here," he ordered and the thralls threw the General to the ground at his feet. He smiled evilly and spat at Evans while the figure struggled to his feet.

"I hope the master lets me deal with you personally," he gloated.

"I doubt we'll get that far," Evans replied and produced a grenade hidden in his sock. The Lieutenant's face went ashen when he saw Evans pull the pin and jump at him. The three vampires arrived and began to metamorphose.

The Lieutenant screamed and felt Evans clamp his hand around his neck and saw him look deep into his eyes. "Join me in Hell," he stated and then the grenade exploded.

The three vampires were caught by the blast, but it wasn't nearly enough to kill any of them. They reeled from the shock when shrapnel tore into their bodies and caused intense pain, but they recovered quickly and set upon the only mortals left.

"What is going on here?" Nero demanded and the Sergeant cowered beneath his baleful glare.

"Father, they're getting closer," Dan Harrington screamed as he glanced down at the priest.

"Nearly finished," Reilly muttered distractedly. He finished the blessing by making the sign of the cross over the well with some chrism. The cool water rippled when the priest sprayed the small vial across its surface. The well was situated at the bottom of the tower, leading some of the residents to speculate that the whole tower was there purely to collect rainwater and ensure a supply for cave residents.

"Father!" Harrington shouted again. His voice climbed several octaves while he watched the swarm of vampires begin their descent.

"Okay, we're done," Reilly shouted back. He pulled the cord on the motor that sat beside the well. The motor roared to life, then spluttered and died. "Shit!" Reilly blasphemed and offered a silent prayer before he pulled the cord again. This time the motor roared and then settled down to a constant hum while it sucked the water through the hose attached to it. The hose ran from the well all the way to the top where Harrington stood. Reilly watched while the hose hardened as gallons of water were forced upward.

When Harrington felt the hose straighten in his grip, filled with water, he reached forward and opened the valve. Water shot out of the nozzle at tremendous force and arched out from the tower into the night air. The tower, while connected to the house, was not actually accessible from the dwelling. The only way in was through the Cave. On the outside it resembled a small circular turret that reached to the same height as the chimney.

Harrington had no idea what its planned use was, but was happy it was here. He planted his feet firmly on the ground and struggled to control the hose.

"Father," he shouted through gritted teeth, "this thing is bucking like a son of a bitch!"

Father Reilly climbed the narrow steps as quickly as he could to help. Together, the two men slowly regained control over the flailing hose and directed the water at the vampires.

"I hope this works," Harrington shouted over the thunderous noise.

"So do I," said Reilly and he held grimly on.

The water shot out into the night and struck the lead vampire with full force. The power sent it reeling back through the swarm. Harrington could see shock register on its face when it looked down at its chest. Gaping holes appeared where the water had hit the creature, and flesh melted away from bone. The creature opened its mouth to scream, but water had splashed onto its throat and destroyed the flesh there. The Vampire fell to the ground in silence.

Harrington grinned while he directed the stream of water from side to side, searing flesh from bone on contact.

Vampires started to fall from the sky; their bodies burned to an unrecognisable mess of bone and withered flesh. The first wave of vampires faltered as those at the back reacted. Bodies veered wildly to avoid the deadly stream.

Vampires crashed into each other in their panic. Their wickedly sharp talons raked deep furrows into each other, while water burned through wings and sent them spiraling to the ground.

Harrington and Reilly whooped for joy as the attack faltered and then broke completely apart.

"Not so tough now are you, motherfuckers?" Harrington shouted, and then sheepishly looked at Reilly. "Sorry, Father."

And then, suddenly, the hose went limp and the water ran out.

CHAPTER
TWENTY- SEVEN

Nero grew angry watching the mayhem. Already six vampires lay dead; their bodies still smouldering from the holy water. Five more lay on the ground holding stumps of arms or legs. They screamed piteously. There was little blood because the water had cauterised the wounds on contact, but it still ate into the flesh that remained like acid. The remaining vampires began to land before him and transform. Flesh rippling over bone and their bat-like features moulded back to human.

"What are you doing back here?" he screamed at them. "You are Vampires, Lords of this earth. Get back up there or I'll destroy you myself!"

The Vampires hesitated, looked from Nero to the house and back again, as if weighing up which they feared most. It wasn't until they noticed that the thunderous sound of the water cannon had stopped that they seemed to be able to choose.

"They've run out." Nero smiled evilly. "Come, follow me. I'll show you what it is to be a Vampire."

With that Nero transformed and launched himself into the air and the remaining swarm followed.

The corridor between the living quarters and the main entrance was a hive of activity. People formed a line and carried tables, chairs, desks and anything else they could find to build a barricade between themselves and the door. The barrier reached almost to the ceiling and stretched at least ten feet in width across the full length of the corridor.

"Come on, people, let's move it; they'll be here soon!" Harris shouted from halfway up the rampart. His voice echoed loudly in the confined space.

"Do you think we can hold them?"

Harris looked down at Sandra Harrington's upturned face. Her eyes, the clearest blue he had ever seen, shone brightly against the background of her dust-encrusted face.

"I really don't know," he sighed. "It depends on how many there are."

Just then Dan Harrington and Father Reilly arrived, both red-faced from the exertion.

"How did it go?" Harris asked.

"We stopped the first wave, but they've already regrouped." Harrington panted between breaths. "Worked like a charm while it lasted, but I never thought all that water would disappear so quickly. How are we fixed here?"

"We're about as ready as we can be. I've set up as many men as I could get behind the barricade with Pat's special ammunition. We still don't know if it'll work but it's all we've got. Father Reilly," Harris addressed the priest, "we've got to get the women and children back to—"

"Sorry, Harris," Reilly interrupted, "you'll have to get someone else. These bastards are about to get their first taste of the wrath of God. I'm staying here." The last words were spoken as the priest lifted a machine gun in his hands and slammed the magazine home. He pulled on the breech, loaded the first round and looked at the others as if daring them to deny him.

Harris gaped at the priest, unsure if he was more surprised at his language or the fact that he looked very comfortable with that weapon. Harris relented with a sigh and looked hopefully at Sandra Harrington.

"Don't even think about it, Peter Harris," she warned. "I'm not being left behind again. This time I'm not leaving your side."

Harris grinned at the look of determination in her face and knew that facing the vampires would be easier than arguing with her.

"All right, but we—"

A heavy boom came from the door. The noise reverberated around the enclosed area and everyone stopped to stare at the door. The door itself was metal, a full seven inches thick and capable of surviving all but a direct hit from a nuclear warhead. Unfortunately, no one had included vampires in the original specifications and the metal was already buckling after the first blow.

"All right, everybody get ready!" Harris shouted and people ran to their positions. "McNamara," the man jumped at the sound of his name. "Get back to the others and help them get out safely!" His face grew serious. "You do realise how important this is, don't you?"

McNamara nodded and sprinted off down the corridor. The air filled with the sound of magazines clicking home and breeches being pulled. Then silence reigned, except for the pounding.

"Hurry up!" Nero screamed at the vampires.

There was room for only three vampires at once at the metal door. Those three had morphed to the fullest, most powerful form they could manage. Only the eldest of the vampires could manage this kind of control, those that had lived at least two hundred years, and Nero had ordered his most trusted lieutenants to the chore.

He smiled and looked upon the three creatures. They each had assumed forms that borrowed heavily from ancient mythology, with an emphasis on power. The first creature, Pollock, had taken the form of a Minotaur and grown to a height of some ten feet. His massive back rippled with muscles as he raised his fists and brought them crashing down against the metal. The second vampire, Narcissus, had sprouted two extra arms and extended its body outward to increase its mass and so maximise its centre of balance. The result allowed the creature to strike the doors with all four appendages and hammer in a constant windmill motion.

The third lieutenant, Thiebes, took a hellish form like nothing even Nero had ever seen. Sticky ochre, the colour of congealed blood, covered its body. Its face was stretched impossibly over a cavern of wickedly sharp teeth. Its red eyes were set deep into its angular head. The creature pivoted back on its short arms and brought its massive legs crashing into the door in a seesaw motion.

The concentration and energy needed to assume and retain these forms was phenomenal. All three would need to feed immediately after they broke through. Indeed, they would need to gorge on the humans to recover from such exertions.

Still, thought Nero, there's plenty to go around.

The noise was unbearable. The constant hammering made everyone flinch with each impact. Harris looked over at Rodgers and Reiss, both men injured with their legs in bandages, but adamant that they would not slow down the escape party. Rodgers caught Harris's eye and winked, a stupid, wide grin transforming his features for a few seconds before grim determination took its place. Harris smiled in acknowledgement and shook his head.

Things just wouldn't be the same without him, Harris thought.

Reiss lay propped against the far wall, his leg heavily bandaged. Four machine guns lay against the wall beside him, and a pile of magazines sprawled on the floor in easy reach.

Dan Harrington and Father Reilly crouched together to his left, and just past them Harris could see Pat Smith, the portly, bald-headed chemist upon whose 'magic' bullets all their lives depended. Smith must have sensed Harris' gaze; he glanced over and nodded.

He felt a hand touch his own and broke the gaze to look at Sandra Harrington and smile. She smiled back, but it didn't quite reach her eyes. She looked tired and frightened. He took her hand in both of his and squeezed gently, and then looked along the line at the forty or so men and women. A deep pride swelled in him. No one here had chosen this path, but each and every one of these people was prepared to die to try and give the others the time to escape through the water tower.

While the vampires' attention was centred on the main entrance of the Cave, the rest of the community would make their way through the water tower and out into the forest beyond. They didn't worry about the vampires trying to use that entrance as they had left just enough water in the bottom of the tanks to make any assault impossible for the creatures, even if they found it.

Harris looked at his watch.

Another ten minutes and they'll be clear, he thought.

Only Father Reilly and himself knew about their final, desperate gambit now that Crockett was dead. The knowledge weighed heavily on his shoulders. He had sought and received absolution from Father Reilly earlier, and now kept checking his waist for the small metal box secreted on his belt.

All along the line men and women dried their sweating hands against trousers and occasionally shifted position when muscles cramped. Each person's attention was riveted on the metal door. The pounding continued.

The metal finally split with an ear shattering crash. A tear appeared almost perfectly down the centre. The remains of the door flew to either side and the entire corridor shook when the heavy doors crashed against the walls. People swallowed on dry throats; knuckles went white as they gripped their weapons tighter. From the faint mist of dust and destruction emerged three visions from hell that pushed through the smoke and approached the humans. The barricade had looked strong and unassailable just minutes before, but when Harris looked up at these creatures it now seemed woefully inadequate.

"Steady!" he heard himself croak and he gripped Sandra Harrington's hand tighter. His legs felt less than steady as the creatures thundered closer.

"Steady!" he called again and then, just as the creatures came in line with a mark on the wall, his arm flashed down.

"Now!" he shouted.

CHAPTER
TWENTY- EIGHT

R odgers heard Harris shout and swung his axe against the tail end of the rope held taut to a metal clasp in the wall. The rope was thick and tied securely to ensure it could hold the enormous weight of their last surprise. The rope snaked up the wall, held in place with tacks, until it reached a metal ring set into the ceiling. Attached to this was a hook that held a very large wooden frame in place, flush with the ceiling. The frame stretched across the entire corridor and, before it had been tied in position, had reached down to about three inches from the ground.

The frame had multiple spikes carved into the wood and their points were wickedly sharp. This gambit had worked well in the forest and Rodgers hoped to God that it would stop the three creatures advancing on them now. Fear rose like bile in his throat and he hacked repeatedly at the rope. Sweat seeped into his eyes. He missed a few times and took chunks out of the wall beside him.

Sweat rolled down Harris' back as he watched the creatures get closer. His eyes moved frantically between Rodgers and the creatures like some demented tennis match, and he willed the rope to break. The lead creature, some form of Minotaur, had the longest legs of the three. It cleared the smoke, seemed to notice Rodgers, and stopped suddenly. The other two quickly caught up.

The creature known as Pollock thundered down the corridor in triumph. The energy it had exerted from destroying the door and retaining its form had worked up an appetite that gnawed at him. The hunger, like a physical pain deep in his stomach, was to be savoured; its massive jaws dripped saliva as he anticipated the slaughter to come.

Pollock looked down at the humans crouched in fear behind a pitiful barricade and laughed at their stupidity. Out of the corner of his eye he saw a human to the side of the others frantically strike the wall and he slowed, well aware of how tricky these humans could be.

Fear engulfed Harris when he watched the creature trace the line of rope and then register a change on his face. Harris couldn't read the features, but he reckoned that the creature had worked out what was about to happen. The creature turned to shout a warning, but in the same moment the rope finally separated and Harris heard a whoop of delight from Rodgers.

Freed of the rope, the hook slid easily from the clasp in the ceiling and the frame began its downward descent.

The other vampires held back to allow the three lieutenants the first blood. The air was charged with the expectant carnage that was sure to follow. Nero watched his lieutenants approach the barricade.

Finally, this annoying resistance comes to an end, he thought. His eyes glowed with anticipation. The rest of his brood waited impatiently at the entrance, like puppies straining against a lead. Nero held them back with a glowering look; he wanted to savour this victory. The vampires were impatient, but held their positions reluctantly, each one raising their heads and sniffing the air. The stench of fear was rank in the enclosed area and Nero knew that even his iron will could not hold them once the carnage began and the blood scent reached them. At that stage, though, there would be plenty for all.

Narcissus saw Pollock slow and then stop. His eyes flickered in every direction to discover why he hesitated with such a feast so close before him. He knew there must be good reason and so slowed his own advance. At the same time that Pollock turned to start back toward him, he watched the frame swing down from the ceiling and impale the vampire.

The frame slammed into Pollock with such force that his body was picked up and lifted high as the frame completed its swing. One of the spikes ripped through Pollock's neck muscle, and bright blood pumped outward in great gushes. Narcissus barely had time to react before the frame continued its arc, ripped into his flesh and shattered bone. He felt spikes rip into his shoulder and his left arm go numb as the sheer force of the blow crushed muscle and cartilage. The second nicked his upper thigh and, rather than penetrating the flesh, it tore a ragged, deep furrow along his leg.

The third and final spike tore through his middle, destroying his spleen, colon and stomach on its way. The pain was excruciating and, though he knew he could survive such damage, the wounds would never truly heal.

At the same time the frame ground to a jarring halt and slammed into Thiebes. Narcissus screamed when the added weight of Thiebes slammed into him and dragged against his own body. He fell to the floor and his wounds ripped further when he slipped down the frame. Narcissus looked over Pollock, but the creature wasn't moving.

He heard Thiebes bellow with anger as he pulled himself from the spikes and gripped his leg where a nasty wound bled copiously. Narcissus knew that all three of them would be dead if Pollock had not seen the trap at the last minute. Slowly he began to pull himself from the frame and slumped to the ground, panting. The pain was so intense that it distracted him. The change come upon him and his ruined body slipped back to human form. Agony tore through him, but he savoured it, knowing he would use the pain to focus.

He would allow himself just enough time to heal and then he would enjoy repaying the humans for their trickery.

Nero's grin of triumph slowly melted when he saw the frame drop from the ceiling and slam into his lieutenants. The sheer speed of the trap took him completely by surprise and caused him momentarily to loose control over the other vampires. The heavy, sweet scent of blood filled the enclosed area and sent the other vampires into a frenzy. The sudden relaxing of his control allowed the pack to swarm uncontrollably into the charnel zone.

The scent of blood was so strong that it intoxicated those relatively new vampires that had never experienced a massacre on this scale. They immediately attacked the source of the precious liquid and pounced on the wounded lieutenants, ripping into their torn bodies with wild abandon. Teeth tore into any exposed area and fresh blood gushed into eager throats and splattered everywhere.

Thiebes grabbed two of the attacking vampires, gripped their heads in his massive hands, and tore them from him before he slammed them both against the wall. Their heads were smashed to pulp against the hard surface, and their bodies dropped limply to the floor while Thiebes reached for two more of the frenzied creatures.

Narcissus lay on the ground. Three Vampires descended on him and plunged their teeth into him greedily. The recent excesses of holding his massive form together and the subsequent shock to his system by the frame had obviously left him weak. He didn't even try to stop them as they literally drained him.

Nero recovered from the shock and screamed at them to stop, but his voice was lost in the general melee of screams and growls coming from the corridor. He focused his will and sent out a strong command through the mind link he maintained with his clan. The mental command was so strong that it was like a physical blow. The Vampires all stopped immediately, stunned by the force and disorientated by the unexpected communication.

Thiebes ignored the command, picked up another vampire in his massive arms, and tore it in two. Nero lost his temper and in a blur of motion he appeared beside his lieutenant and reached out to stay his hand when he reached for another.

"Take him down!" he shouted, indicating Pollock. Three vampires rushed to the task. "You fools," he hissed. "*They* are the enemy," his arm shot out and pointed at the barricade and the humans behind it.

Harris was at a loss to explain the carnage that erupted after the frame had come down, but was delighted to see the Vampires fighting among themselves. One of the older creatures was definitely dead. The other two were injured, although how badly he couldn't tell. At least twenty other Vampires were left, including Nero.

"Damn!" Harris muttered when he saw the creatures stop their infighting and turn their attention on the humans. One of the larger creatures, the one covered in a dark red, almost claret, sticky substance, leaned back on its massive arms and kicked at the frame. He shattered it with one kick. Harris ducked down as splinters and shards of wood flew at the barricade and ricocheted off the metal in a dangerous hail. Some people grunted as wood cut flesh and ripped into muscle. Harris glanced up and down the line to ascertain the damage and saw numerous people holding limbs, but no serious injuries. He sighed with relief and then saw the hoard advance.

"Heads up people!" he shouted. "Here they come!"

CHAPTER
TWENTY–NINE

The Vampires descended on the barricade in a swarm, snarling and growling their hatred. The sheer speed and ferocity of their attack took many of the humans by surprise; some of them actually dropped their weapons and backed away from the barrier. The remaining humans frantically tried to stretch their numbers further along the line to make up for the gaps. Harris could see their fear. They shifted their gaze from him to the approaching creatures and back again, waiting for the signal.

The creatures moved unbelievably quickly and crossed the distance in no time. They were nearly on top of the barricade. Guns started to slip in palms slick with sweat. Still Harris stood with his hand raised. It wasn't until the first slavering creature actually touched the far edge of the barrier that Harris dropped his arm and the humans finally let loose a devastating hail of fire on the creatures.

The first volley of fire slammed into them like a wall and stopped them dead in their tracks. The lead Vampires laughed when the bullets hit them, but then uncertainty replaced their original confidence. Pain registered on their faces, a hot searing pain that remained long after it should have. The bullets continued to fly and the enclosed corridor stank with cordite. The force of the bullets pushed the Vampires back and their bodies jerked spasmodically with each impact.

The five leading vampires took the brunt of the barrage and their bodies were riddled with bleeding holes. The humans who had initially dropped their weapons could now see that the vampires were being forced back. Encouraged, they began to filter back, pick up their weapons and add to the carnage.

"Hold your fire!" Harris screamed until he was hoarse when he saw the vampires fall back. Sporadic fire continued for a few more minutes and some people, deafened by the noise, had to be shaken by their colleagues to bring them back to reality.

The silence in the corridor was eerie and the smoke from the gunfire only added to the gothic atmosphere.

"Did the bullets work?"

Harris' ears were still ringing from the noise. He barely heard Sandra Harrington's question.

"I don't know!" he shouted his reply. "We pumped so many rounds into them that even normal bullets would have driven them back. We'll have to see if they heal."

Nero fumed while he looked down at the creatures that had led the charge. "What's wrong with them?" he bellowed. "Why don't they heal?" His voice had a touch of desperation about it and the other creatures shifted uncomfortably at this lack of confidence.

The creatures, six in all, were horribly deformed. The sheer force of the bullets had torn flesh from their bodies; bloody, oozing holes covered their torsos. Normally these wounds would have already begun to heal, but the flesh around the open wounds was still burning and the smell of charred flesh was heavy in the air.

Two of the creatures were already dead, agony frozen on their faces. The other four looked dead. An occasional movement or groan was the only indication that they were still conscious. Nero had never seen vampires so weak and his mind was in turmoil.

This new development scared him.

Vampires were immortal, created to rule this pitiful planet and all its inhabitants. It was bad enough that they had a weakness for wooden stakes and holy water, but a smart vampire easily avoided these. Bullets, however, were a different story completely. The sheer scope of the problem nearly overwhelmed him and his indecision was having a negative effect on the other vampires.

Nero straightened to his full height. He had made his decision. These humans must be destroyed no matter the cost. The alternative, if they survived, was incomprehensible. This new weapon could see the tide turn for humans. They might regain their dominant position on the earth and that could not be allowed to happen.

"Thiebes!" he shouted, confidence again oozing from his erect figure. "This new development cannot be allowed to go any further. It must end here. Do you understand what I am saying?" Nero looked straight at his lieutenant as he spoke.

Thiebes nodded his understanding, bent down to two of the dying vampires and lifted them easily. He draped them over his shoulder, settled them in position to cover his vital organs, and looked one final time as his master. He nodded and then pounded back down the corridor toward the barricade.

Harris felt the thump of the approaching vampire long before he saw him. The massive figure suddenly came into view and Harris blanched at its sheer size. He had only caught glimpses of the ancient creatures before the frame had slammed into them, and the distance had made them seem less impressive. This creature, however, was still thirty feet away and already seemed to fill the entire corridor. He looked down the line and could see the terror in his people's faces. Each powerful step that rumbled down the corridor caused everyone to cringe as they watched in fascination as death itself approached.

Harris snapped out of his terror with an almost physical wrench. He could see that everyone was literally petrified, unable to attack or even to turn and run away.

Twenty-five feet.

Desperately Harris raised his weapon and shouted, "Pour it into the bastard!"

Then he opened fire. The recoil slammed into his shoulder repeatedly. Bullets flew across the short space and impacted with dull thuds. The noise of the shout and the hammering of the machine gun seemed to break the spell. People along the line shook themselves and one by one they all raised the weapons and began to fire.

Twenty Feet.

The bullets flew in a merciless hail. They burned when they hit and Thiebes felt the agony of round after round that hit home. The two vampires he used as shields took the brunt of the attack, but many bullets hit home. Any unprotected area was a target and his legs, arms and neck were on fire with agony. The sheer force of the attack began to slow his advance as more and more bullets slammed into him. He steeled himself and lowered his head, closed his eyes and bellowed his rage as he put his remaining strength into a last effort.

Fifteen Feet.

Harris saw the creature falter. Fingers froze on triggers; people dropped empty magazines, loaded new ones and continued firing in a daze. Shell cases flew everywhere. Men and women stood in a sea of spent cartridges. People dropped their machine guns and picked up new ones when they overheated or jammed.

Ten Feet.

Harris stopped firing to let his weapon cool down and looked worriedly at the rapidly dwindling pile of Pat Smith's 'magic' bullets.

Oh well, it won't matter if we don't stop this guy, he thought and, despite himself and their situation, he felt a grudging respect for the creature's magnificent effort against such devastating force.

The creature began to stumble.

"We've no more treated ammunition." He felt the tug on his sleeve and looked down at Sandra Harrington.

"Just use the normal stuff, but keep firing."

The whole corridor shook as the creature fell to one knee. The bodies of the dead vampires he had used as shields slid to the ground, their forms no longer recognisable. The humans immediately pumped rounds into the creature's exposed chest and the creature finally slumped forward with a final howl of defiance.

The creature was already dead when it fell, so it was unaware that its final act would have such important ramifications. Its massive body fell forward and its outstretched hand came down right in the middle of the barrier. The force of the limb crushed the metal of the barrier. Two men were sent spinning into the air and vaulted out into the corridor. They landed heavily and sat dazed for a few moments while they recovered.

The limb had left a gaping hole in the humans' defenses and the vampires were quick to react. As one they swarmed on the hapless humans, whose screams stopped abruptly when the creatures swamped them.

This time the assault was blindingly quick and the humans were not prepared for it. The barrage of bullets, when it finally began, was sporadic and lacked the power of the previous defense.

The vampires felt the bullets strike their bodies, but these wounds didn't burn like the others and they could feel the wounds heal almost as quickly as they struck. They pounced on the barricade and ripped at the metal to get at the humans. Many of the metal tables and chairs had been welded together for added strength, which delayed the vampires at first. High-pitched squeals filled the air as metal was ripped apart and razor claws gutted humans when the vampires pushed through.

Five vampires swamped the gap left by Thiebes, and the others attacked the structure itself. Rodgers saw the danger, immediately grabbed the defenders next to him, and pulled them with him to defend the breech. The vampires were so fast that, before they got to the gap, one made it through, jumped at the lone defender, and ripped his head clean from his shoulders in one motion.

Rodgers had brought four men with him. Two went down almost immediately when the vampire pirouetted gracefully and gutted both with its sharp claws. Rodgers still had the axe he had used earlier. He swung the weapon with all his strength when the vampire prepared to launch another attack. The blade flew through the air and struck the vampire in the side of the head. The axe split its skull with a load crack and the creature dropped dead to the floor. Rodgers was caught off balance by the blow and unable to defend himself from the second vampire. He felt himself thrown into the air and struck the wall with such force that the crack of breaking bone was audible even over the noise of the battle.

More men began to arrive at the breech. Two vampires had made it through now, and dead bodies were strewn everywhere. The lead vampire reached for the first human, but had over-stretched and slipped on a pool of blood. It fell to the ground and tried vainly to get back to its feet, but the humans threw down their now useless guns and hacked and prodded the creature with wooden stakes, spears and any other weapons they could find. More reinforcements arrived and pushed back against the other invading vampires. Slowly but surely their very numbers forced the creatures back.

Harris saw Rodgers thrown from the breach and strike the wall. His heart sank when he saw the limp form slide to the ground, but then a creature suddenly appeared before him. It rocked slightly as it fought to regain its balance on the barrier's unstable surface. Harris was distracted momentarily when he heard a scream. He looked down to see Sandra Harrington fall to the ground with blood spurting from a wound at her neck.

Harris threw his machine gun down and ripped a machete from its holster at his side. The rage he felt was like a jolt of adrenaline and he swung at the creature before him. The blow was badly aimed, but the sheer force behind it cleaved the creature's skull in two. Desperate to get to Sandra, Harris hacked and slashed his way through the arms which poked through the failing barrier and finally gained a gap. He dropped down and turned her prone form to see how badly she had been hurt.

"Thank God," he sighed when he saw the gaping wound at her shoulder and realised the wound was not fatal. "Dan!" he shouted and grabbed the older man." Gather up half those that are left and take up position behind the next barrier. Bring the wounded with you and we'll hold them as long as possible." He shoved Sandra's unconscious body into her father's arms." Take care of her," he said. Dan Harrington seemed to hesitate. "Move!" Harris shouted. Harrington seemed to shake himself and then ran along the line, taking every second defender.

Harris watched while half his force limped back toward the final barrier further down the corridor. The vampires had slackened their assault and they paused to take stock. Bodies littered the ground and hung at impossible angles across the remaining pieces of the barrier. Twelve humans lay dead. Five vampires had been destroyed, leaving both sides about equal in number, if not in power.

The remaining humans, some twenty people, steeled themselves for the next assault. Father Reilly caught Harris' eye and smiled. His face was covered in blood and his grin looked maniacal. The vampires seemed to sense the weakening of the defenses and began to shuffle forward. Just then, everyone, including the vampires, stopped when a pounding noise came from the top of the corridor. Nero appeared and grinned like a Cheshire cat. Behind him loomed the massive form of Pollock.

Oh Shit! thought Harris.

CHAPTER
THIRTY

T he vampires attacked en masse and with such ferocity that the humans couldn't hope to stop them. Vampires poured through the gap, scaled over the top of the barrier, and ripped flesh with their claws and teeth. Men and women fell and blood splattered everywhere. The coppery smell of the blood only sent the creatures further into frenzy.

Father Reilly panted with the exertion. He swung a wooden spear and impaled yet another creature. Its scream sent a shiver down his spine, but he had no time to gloat. He had carved the spear to a sharp point at either end, which made it easier to use in close combat. He pulled the weapon from the dead creature and continued the arc backwards to impale a second creature attacking from behind.

There's too many, he thought as yet another appeared through the gap. He pulled the spear from the dead vampire, but this creature was too quick. It grabbed the weapon and pulled it easily from his grasp.

"Oh, I'm sorry, Father. Did you want it back?" the creature mocked and then spun the weapon faster than Reilly could hope to follow. The point drove straight through Reilly's chest. The creature's strength forced the spear out through his back and continued on through most of the weapon's six-foot length. The spear nearly touched the ground behind him and left about six inches sticking from his chest.

"Now you know what it feels like, priest. It hurts, doesn't it?" the creature spat.

Reilly felt the strength leave his legs and stumbled forward. The creature laughed and leaned in to rip the priest's throat out and gorge on his blood. Reilly's vision began to blur and the reek of the creature's breath filled his nostrils.

"Why don't you tell me?" Reilly said.

The priest grunted, grabbed the creature by its shoulders and, before it could react, pulled the vampire to him and impaled it on the protruding spear. The vampire screamed in agony, and then both of them fell to the ground, locked in an eternal embrace.

Reiss sat on the barrier and sprayed holy water at any vampires that came within range. His leg was useless from his earlier fall, but the water gave him enough range to keep the creatures at bay for now. His supply, however, was dwindling rapidly.

Another creature lunged at him and he flicked the bottle toward it, spraying a fine mist in its direction. The creature screamed as the liquid burned a line across its face. Its left eye melted on contact. Pain seared into the vampire's skull and it thrashed blindly into the melee. Its frenzied flight caught another vampire by mistake and gauged deep furrows across the creature's face before the blinded vampire was brought down by its own kind in a brief but violent exchange.

"Hey, don't mind me," Reiss quipped. "Feel free to tear each other to pieces. I'll just sit here and watch."

The vampires growled their response, but kept their distance. Reiss smiled confidently, but he knew that the water wouldn't last much longer.

"Let me go!" Sandra Harrington screamed and fought against her father. They had made it back to the second barricade long before she had regained consciousness, allowing her father the opportunity to clean and dress her wound. The second barrier was merely a ragged line built with any materials they had left over from the main barricade. It wasn't really meant to stop the vampires, but it had given the men something to do while they waited for the assault to begin.

Sandra had woken with a start and immediately looked about her. She saw the relative calm around her and looked at her father questioningly. "What happened?" she asked. Her voice rose as realisation hit her. "Where is he?" she asked without waiting for a response to her previous question.

"He told us to come back here and wait for him. You were injured..." Dan Harrington stopped halfway through his explanation, knowing that it wouldn't do any good. "Look Sandra," he put his hands firmly on her shoulders and looked directly into her eyes, "we left them at least ten minutes ago and the gunfire stopped five minutes after that. We..."

"No!" she screamed. "Let me go!" She pulled away from her father and thumped her fists against his chest while the tears streamed down her face. "He promised we wouldn't separate this time, he promised...!"

Her father reached out and folded her in his arms, comforting her while she wept.

Rodgers stirred. His head felt like it had been slammed into a wall. Then he remembered that was exactly what had happened. He rolled over, opened his eyes, and suddenly came fully awake.

"Oh my God!" he muttered when he saw the carnage in front of him.

The creature swiped at Harris and tore the flesh of his right arm from elbow down to his wrist. The sudden pain made him drop the machete. The creature grinned evilly and took its time advancing on its helpless prey. Harris looked around frantically for something to protect himself and made a grab for a piece of metal sticking out of the barrier. His hand had just closed on the bar when he felt it ripped from his grasp. He looked up and saw the Minotaur creature lift the entire barrier up and fling it with ease back down the corridor.

"He's mine," the monster growled.

Harris paled as the creature reached for him and he braced himself for the attack. Suddenly, from behind him, Harris heard an almighty roar and watched in disbelief while the creature's head and most of his upper torso disappeared in a spray of blood and bone. The attack was so sudden and so devastating that all fighting stopped and everyone watched the giant, headless creature sway and then collapse to the floor.

Humans and vampires continued to stare at the corpse in utter shock, unable to move until a loud yell drew their attention back down the corridor. Harris couldn't believe his eyes. A smile spread across his face when he recognised the figure.

"Warkowski!" he whispered, "you beautiful bastard."

Warkowski stood some twenty feet away; his body covered in bandages, holding the biggest damn machine gun Harris had ever seen. "Alright, unless you bastards want some of the same," he warned, "I suggest you all just cool it and move on back a bit."

Warkowski's voice carried easily. Harris could see the vampires look uncertainly at their leader.

Nero looked at the devastated remains of Pollock and then back at the huge weapon in Warkowski's arms.

"I said move back!" Warkowski shouted and let loose a short burst at the closest vampire. The bullets that slammed into the creature tore it clean in half. "There's plenty more left if you want some," he warned with the weapon pointed at Nero.

Nero nodded quickly at the rest of his pack and they hurriedly withdrew.

Harris and the remaining humans quickly gathered up those unable to walk and made their way over behind Warkowski. Harris' eyes scanned the many dead men and women around him and sighed deeply at the loss. Two men lifted Reiss in their arms and carried him forward. Just as he was about to leave, Harris noticed movement from a crumpled form over by the wall.

"I don't suppose there's any chance of a beer?" Rodgers smiled. Harris rushed over to help his friend.

"It's just as well you hit the wall with your head," Harris commented when he saw the trickle of blood still seeping from a wound on his forehead, "nothing major there to damage."

Rodgers' smile grew into a grin.

"What are you waiting for, Warkowski? Let them have it." Harris came up behind Warkowski and nodded toward the remaining vampires. The men faced the vampires over a gap of twenty feet, while the vampires looked warily at the massive machine gun in the big man's hands. Most of the other survivors had already started back to the other barrier.

"Ah, bit of a problem there, I'm afraid." Warkowski grinned.

"What do you mean?" Rodgers asked and hobbled up beside him.

"Well, I was trying to make a big impact, you understand," he continued and then nodded at the huge gun in his arms. "Only problem being there wasn't much in the way of ammunition and—"

"But you said there was plenty left." Harris fought to keep his voice low.

"Well, I, ah, exaggerated a bit." Warkowski shrugged.

"When you say a bit—"

"Well, a lot actually. I used my last rounds to kill that vampire over there."

The vampires were beginning to mutter among themselves and inch forward.

"You're mad, you know that, don't you? Stark raving mad!" Harris exclaimed and eyed the vampires. "I think we've just been rumbled. On my mark I suggest we get the hell out of here."

The others nodded.

"Okay, RUN!"

CHAPTER
THIRTY-ONE

"Leave me here, God damn it!" Reiss shouted at the two men who carried him. "You won't make it if you have to drag me. I'll never be able to climb out of here anyway."

The two men looked uncertainly at each other.

"Come on, guys," Reiss persisted, "if you leave me close to the armoury at least I can take some of the bastards with me."

The three of them had set off with the others while Warkowski held the vampires at bay. The other humans had disappeared at this stage, and the two men—Reiss didn't even know their names—were struggling with the extra weight. Reiss could tell they were torn between fear for their own safety and loyalty to him. They kept looking back the way they had come and he knew that they'd drop him the instant the vampires appeared. They didn't need much encouragement and immediately made for a doorway a short distance further on up the corridor.

"Okay, drop me here and leave your grenades. I'll set up a little surprise for our friends."

"Well, if you're sure…" the second man muttered and found it hard not to show his relief.

They left Reiss sitting on a box of ammunition with a collection of grenades around him. He had positioned himself at an angle to the door, which gave him a view back down the corridor. *At least I'll see them coming,* he thought.

The two men left quickly. Neither one was able to look Reiss in the eye when they hurried out of the room.

Can't really blame them, he thought and readied himself.

The men ran down the corridor, but the vampires gained rapidly. Rodgers limped badly and Harris literally had to pull him along, supporting him as best he could. Warkowski supported his other side. Between them they dragged the injured man down the corridor.

With only a twenty-foot advantage, it wouldn't be long before the vampires caught up with them. They ran expecting to feel sharp claws rake their backs at any second. Harris had no idea what they were going to do even if they did make it to the barrier. There wasn't time to plan anything and they were out of the 'magic' bullets. There was no way to delay the creatures any further.

He hoped Sandra had made it out.

Reiss watched the three men struggle along the corridor. The vampires were right behind them; he could see about ten of them from where he sat. In fact, the creatures looked as though they were keeping station behind the men, rather than actually trying to catch them.

Like a mouse playing with its prey, Reiss thought. He judged the distance to the struggling men and performed a quick calculation. He offered a silent prayer, and then reached down and pulled the pins on the grenades in his lap and lay back.

I hope I've timed this right.

Harris knew that the vampires were playing. They taunted them and leaned forward to swipe at exposed flesh. Then they withdrew, only to catch up and swipe again. They knew that they had won, that the humans had finally run out of surprises, and they were enjoying their victory. Long scratches of varying depths covered Harris' back, but he continued on in the vain hope that something might happen.

And then, suddenly, it did.

The explosion ripped apart the whole wall to their right. The force picked the three men up and threw them further down the corridor, where they crashed heavily in a jumbled heap. The force of the explosion completely decimated the wall and most of the ceiling.

Debris and dust covered Harris. He lay curled in a ball as the shrapnel continued to fall. The noise of the explosion was deafening in the close confines of the corridor, and his ears rang painfully while he struggled to his feet. He looked around and saw both Warkowski and Rodgers stir, but could see no sign of the vampires.

His leg hurt. He looked down to see a small sliver of metal protruding from his thigh. "God, will this night ever end?" he pleaded out loud before he pulled at the shrapnel. He checked the wound and nodded when he saw that it wasn't bleeding badly. He turned to see what had happened and saw that the roof had caved in behind them, completely blocking the corridor.

Realisation came slowly, but when it did, a low chuckle rose in his throat. By the time Rodgers had limped up behind him, he was laughing and holding his side with the pain that lanced through his battered body.

"What's so funny?" Rodgers asked.

"They were caught on the other side," he managed between fits of laughter. Rodgers joined in, the relief from this short reprieve made them laugh all the more.

"We better move, that won't keep them long." Warkowski broke up the party. The other two sobered fast and set off toward the barrier.

Dan Harrington supervised the retreat. They had waited as long as they dared and must now look to the living. The unexpected arrival of some of the defenders, with news of Warkowski's rescue, had buoyed the spirits of the small party. Hope had soared that they might actually get a few more out alive.

Harrington had left his daughter and moved to organise the retreat. Sandra ran to each of the survivors and questioned each one. Her questions became more desperate as the line of men and women grew shorter.

The door to the tower was set into the wall behind them. Dan supervised, while people lined up and went through in single file. The tower measured some twenty-five feet in diameter and contained a walled circle that ran around the circumference. The wall began about six inches into the tower and rose to about four feet in height. Inside the enclosure was a pool of water about three feet in depth. At the far side of the tower a series of metal rungs traced a line up the entire height of the tower.

The survivors waded through the water and began to climb. Harrington looked up and judged the climb to be some two hundred feet straight up, and then another fifty or so back down on the outside to reach the ground. He glanced up, frowned at the brightening sky, and looked at his watch.

My God, he thought, *we've fought all night.*

"All right, people," he said aloud, "let's make all this effort worth something. It's time to get out of here."

Harris and his two colleagues rounded the corner and saw the barrier. He looked quickly behind him and could see no sign of the vampires. His heart beat faster and hope began to grow. "Come on," he urged the others, "not far now."

Nero fidgeted while his pack cleared the debris. He fumed that he hadn't beheaded the humans when he had the chance, but his pride had demanded retribution and he had enjoyed the chase. "Next time," he vowed, "I will rip them to shreds and take my time over their carcasses."

He marveled at the humans' ingenuity. Twenty vampires dead. He shook his head. He would not have thought they could kill one of his kind, let alone twenty, and he itched to finish this embarrassment. The vampires were too slow for him and, with a bellow of rage, he grabbed several creatures, threw them aside, and attacked the debris. His great strength pulverised rock and produced a hole in the barrier in seconds.

"Now," he shouted, "tear them to pieces!"

And the remaining creatures flooded through.

The three men had reached the tower door when they heard the scream of triumph back down the corridor.

"Come on, hurry," Harris encouraged the other two men. He pulled open the door and ushered them inside. Harris followed and immediately looked for a means to secure the door. The door lock was a simple one that would not hold the vampires for long. He turned the key and told Warkowski and Rodgers to begin climbing, then he dragged the pump machine that Reilly had used earlier in front of the metal door.

Grunting with the effort, Harris dropped the machine flush with the door and nodded.

That'll have to do, he thought and then glanced upwards. Warkowski and Rodgers were already a quarter of the way up and further past them he could see some of the others near the top.

"Thank God," he whispered, "at least Sandra is safe."

The first loud clang against the metal door reverberated around the tower as he began to climb.

The door exploded inward with such force that it landed clear across the far side of the tower. The vampires poured in so swiftly that those in the lead failed to realise that there was an enclosure until the pain began to register. They waded into the water and then suddenly stopped. They howled as the blessed water seeped through their clothes and began to burn like acid. Flesh and bone melted away in seconds; the creatures lost their balance and fell into the water. The screams intensified as arms, knees and faces were the next to touch the water. The pitiful creatures howled while their bodies decomposed in the cool water until, finally, they slumped forward and slid beneath the surface.

The other vampires had barely enough time to see the trap and paused at the door to change to their bat forms. When they were ready, they rose into the air and flew after the escaping humans. Halfway up, they felt the prickly sensation of the dawn's light and screamed when the faint light began to burn their bodies.

Small pockets of flame appeared on the lead vampires. One by one they fell to the ground. Two vampires fell into the pool and thrashed wildly when the blessed water immediately seared their thin wings and destroyed them in seconds. Another vampire tried to continue flying despite the flames, but suddenly erupted into a fireball and fell in a smouldering heap in the corner.

Nero felt the prickly sensation of the light, but his skin was much tougher than the newer vampires. He looked up and saw Harris near the top. The frustrations of this whole debacle consumed him and he screamed at his hated foe. That man had done this and he would pay.

Heedless of the pain that seared through him, he continued up into the light and forced his body to grow and mutate while he shot upwards. His wings expanded until they reached across the entire tower. His features changed, his lips drew further back, teeth grew and his skin became scaled to protect against the light.

The few fires that had appeared on his body grew smaller and went out as the tougher skin covered the exposed flesh. He grinned grotesquely as he neared his prey.

Harris hurried as fast as he could. The sweat on his palms made him slip occasionally, but slowly he neared the top. He looked down and saw Nero approaching with the speed of a freight train. He glanced quickly upward. He still had some twenty rungs to go.

Too far.

He felt the wind from the vampire's wings draught past him as it loomed closer.

Fifteen rungs.

And then he felt a searing pain in his back when Nero slashed at him. His grip loosened and he almost fell. Blindly, he reached upward and felt cold metal with his right hand. He gripped frantically and swung precariously from the ladder, while he flailed his left hand out to steady himself. He knocked against the wall and used the momentum to grip the rung more tightly, and finally got his other hand onto the ladder. He heard a deep laugh and closed his eyes while he braced for another blow.

Nero laughed and swung a killing blow at the helpless human, but, suddenly, he felt a sharp pain in his chest. He looked down and saw a long wooden spear protruding from the centre of his chest, left of his heart. Puzzled, he glanced upward to locate the source of this latest attack, and then felt himself lifted away from the human and hauled out into the sunlight.

Harris saw the creature rush past him and disappear out over the lip of the tower. Relief flowed through him. He gathered up the last of his energy and hurried onward.

Steele strained as he levered the vampire out into the daylight. He planted the end of the spear against the tower's edge to support the weight of the creature, and sent it sprawling down to the ground below. Freed of the spear, Steele quickly wrapped his hands with his jacket, gripped the outside of the ladder and shot down to the ground below. He used his legs to slow his descent and quickly turned to face the vampire while it still struggled to its feet.

"You!" Nero shrieked. He disdainfully ripped the spear from his body and threw it at Steele, who pivoted to the side. The spear embedded itself into the tower wall. The sun had moved higher in the sky and its heat bathed the adversaries. Small pockets of flame began to appear all over Nero's body.

"That must be painful," Steele commented with a grin as the flames spread.

The blue flame that licked over Nero's flesh created the impression of an aura around him. Flesh puckered and flaked. The creature's healing process created new flesh beneath that, before it too began to burn and then heal. The process was agonising, but not fatal to the ancient vampire, who looked at Steele balefully.

"I told you before, human," he hissed "this pathetic light is not enough to kill one as old as I. You will die for this."

He launched himself at Steele, slammed into his chest and took both of them to the ground.

The proximity to the flames burnt the very air in his throat and Steele gagged when he drew breath. He tried to pull away, but was too late. The creature grabbed him and the flames seared his arms when the creature threw him across the clearing. In a blur the vampire had crossed to where Steele lay and reached down for him. The other humans watched the two figures struggle in shock. They were completely at a loss to explain what was happening.

Rodgers shook himself from the paralysis and ran to help Steele. He had no idea who the man was; he had already been at the base of the tower when the survivors had descended. He hadn't said a word, just stood waiting until the last of the party had jumped to the ground. Without a word he pulled a wickedly sharp spear from the ground beside him and proceeded to climb to the top. He obviously knew Nero, but he was human, and that was enough for Rodgers.

Rodgers took off his jacket and wrapped it around his hands while he ran. He grabbed the vampire. His hands burned even through the heavy fabric, but he wrenched the creature off the struggling human.

Nero spun, backhanded Rodgers and sent him crashing against the tower wall. The distraction had been enough, however, and Steele took the opportunity to overbalance the vampire and slide out from under him.

Rodgers lay gasping for breath at the base of the tower when Harris jumped the last few feet to the ground beside him. "Go, help him," he croaked.

Harris ran at Nero, caught the vampire low and carried him away from the blond man. They tumbled toward the group. Rodgers pulled himself to his knees and noticed that the others had begun to join the fray.

Dan Harrington was the first to reach the vampire. He swung at the creature. Nero moved quickly and easily dodged the blow. Then he reached forward and grabbed the overbalanced human by the arm. The creature turned him around and pulled him tightly against his chest to use as a shield. Flame seared into Harrington's back. The other humans backed off.

Rodgers could see the vampire smile and then, without warning, he traced a claw across Harrington's neck. A thin red line appeared under Harrington's chin, then a few trickles, and finally a deluge poured from his throat. Rodgers looked on helplessly as the creature leaned down and viciously ripped into Harrington's throat before he discarded the body. The flames that had raged all over the creature's body flickered and then died.

"Noooo!" Sandra Harrington screamed as her father crumpled to the ground.

Rodgers could see her glare at the vampire with pure hatred. Suddenly she ran at Nero. Her reaction was so quick that he hadn't expected it and never came close to stopping her. She crossed the short distance in a blur and slammed into the creature, her momentum enough to overbalance the vampire and force it backward.

Rodgers ran after her and tried to get her to break off, but she was oblivious to everything around her. The creature's skin still hissed from the heat of the flames, but she pummeled the vampire, heedless of the pain. Rodgers gained on them and saw the spear lodged in the wall scant seconds before the two slammed against it. He fell to his knees as they both screamed in pain and the spear ripped into both of them.

Harris ran after the struggling pair and howled when the spear ripped through Sandra's back.

She cried out once and then slumped forward against the creature. The vampire bellowed when the spear penetrated its heart. He wrenched the woman away from him and sent her flying backward. Harris saw Sandra driven back and jumped to catch her body and ease her to the ground. He looked down at the blood pouring from the wound and placed his hand against the flow, vainly trying to stop the gushing fluid.

Tears ran down his face, and then the blond stranger appeared at his side. He forced Harris away while he examined the wound. His hands ran knowledgeably over her body and then he tore strips from his own clothes and packed the wound.

Harris looked at her face. So pale, he thought and then felt himself being helped to his feet.

"Come on, buddy, let him work."

He looked up in a daze and saw Rodgers. Blood covered the left side of his face and an ugly bruise had already puffed up the cheekbone, giving him the appearance of a chipmunk. Harris glanced down, saw an axe swinging from a loop on Rodger's belt and, without a word, grabbed the weapon and turned to face the struggling vampire.

The creature lay back against the tower wall with the spear protruding some six feet outward. He was slumped forward and small fires had begun to appear on its body again. The creature looked at Harris.

"So you've come to gloat, human."

"Actually, no," Harris replied and raised the axe.

The creature saw the weapon; Harris saw fear cross its face as the axe descended. Again and again he raised the axe and brought it down on the vampire. Blood spurted and flesh tore until, exhausted, Harris slumped to his knees and the bloodied axe fell from his grasp. The vampire was a bloody mess, sunlight had not yet killed it; the spear through the heart had not been enough to send this ancient creature to hell, but the combination of these things had overloaded its healing ability and, finally, it had begun to die.

The sun had grown in strength over the last few minutes and the creature screamed when its flesh began to melt from its face. Flames flickered over his body and grew in intensity. Flesh blackened and peeled away from the bone. His eyes popped, the liquid within burst in flame and seared into the creature's brain. Its mouth opened to scream, but its tongue shriveled in the heat, and all Harris could hear was a dry rattle before its body slumped forward on the spear and the flames consumed the remains.

Rodgers came forward and touched Harris on the shoulder. "It's over, come on," he urged.

"Just a second," Harris replied. He rose to his feet and approached the blackened corpse, raised the axe one more time, brought it down on the exposed neck and severed the creature's head in one fluid strike. The head fell to the ground at his feet. He raised his boot, brought it down hard on the skull, and shattered the brittle bone.

"Just to be sure," he nodded at Rodgers and allowed himself to be led back to the group.

"She was lucky," Steele began. "An inch lower and she'd be dead. As it stands, it'll be a while before she's up and around. She lost a lot of blood, so her body will have to replace that before she can really heal."

"Thank you," Harris leaned forward and shook Steele's hand. "Who did you say you were again?"

"The name's Steele."

"Harris," the other replied.

The two men smiled at each other, but Steele could see the suspicion in the other's eyes.

"You, ah, knew him?" Harris fumbled the question and nodded toward the creature's corpse.

"Yeah, I used to work for him." Steele met Harris' gaze evenly.

"Why the sudden change of heart?" Harris asked.

"Well, a colleague of mine showed me that there's a difference between existing and living. I decided to try living."

"Good for you. Any plans?" Harris ventured.

"No, not yet. You?" Steele replied.

"Oh, I thought we'd clear up here, then go into town and start weaning the rest of the city off that damned serum. After that we'll move on to the next city, then the next. After that, who knows?"

"That's a mighty tall order," Steele commented.

"That it is."

"There might be pockets of thralls left in the city," Steele ventured.

"We can handle them."

Steele looked over at the bedraggled band of humans dubiously. There were fifteen in total, all injured to some degree. "I know a shortcut," he said, then looked into Harris' eyes.

After a second Harris grinned. "I thought you'd never offer."

Both men laughed and turned back toward the small group.

LaVergne, TN USA
02 November 2009

162756LV00002B/69/A